"McCaffrey's unromanticized portrait of the times is full of muck and grit, and horse lovers and fans of historical fiction will find much to enjoy in the details."
—*Library Journal*

And acclaim for Anne McCaffrey's DRAGONRIDERS OF PERN® series

"Anne McCaffrey, with her dragons, says something very valuable about the interplay of humans and the world around them."
—MARION ZIMMER BRADLEY
Bestselling author of *The Mists of Avalon*

"Few are better at mixing elements of high fantasy and hard science fiction."
—*The New York Times Book Review*

"Not since St. George set off on his quest has there been such a flap over dragons."
—*People*

By Anne McCaffrey
Published by The Ballantine Publishing Group:

BLACK
HORSES
FOR THE
KING

Anne McCaffrey

A Del Rey® Book
THE BALLANTINE PUBLISHING GROUP • NEW YORK

A Del Rey® Book
Published by The Ballantine Publishing Group
Copyright © 1996 by Anne McCaffrey

All rights reserved under International and Pan-American Copyright Conventions. Published in the United States by The Ballantine Publishing Group, a division of Random House, Inc., New York, and simultaneously in Canada by Random House of Canada Limited, Toronto.

Requests for permission to make copies of any part of the work should be mailed to: Permissions Department, Harcourt Brace & Company, 6277 Sea Harbor Drive, Orlando, Florida 32887-6777.

This novel was developed from the author's story "Black Horses for a King," which first appeared in the anthology *Camelot*, edited by Jane Yolen and published by Philomel in 1995.

http://www.randomhouse.com

Library of Congress Catalog Card Number: 98-96288

ISBN 0-345-42257-0

This edition published by arrangement with Harcourt Brace & Co.

Manufactured in the United States of America

First Ballantine Books International Edition: June 1997
First Ballantine Books Trade Paperback Edition: September 1997
First Ballantine Books Domestic Edition: September 1998

10 9 8 7 6 5 4 3 2 1

Apart from their love of Pern,
Marilyn and Harry Alm
are long-term friends and fans,
and thus it is my pleasure
to dedicate this book to them
in appreciation of their many
kindnesses and courtesies over
the years of our association.

GALWYN'S
BRITAIN
c. 500 A.D.

Roman roads connected most
major settlements at the time.

North Sea

Irish Sea

Eburacum

Deva

Viroconium

Metaris Aest

Ratae

Glein

Durobrivae

Glevum

Corinium

Aqua Sulis

Londinium

Camelot

Durnovaria

Sorviodunum

Isca

MILES 50
KILOMETERS 80

A NOTE FROM THE AUTHOR

I ONCE SWORE that I would never write an Arthurian story, as I had many problems with the more commonly known Hollywood version of King Arthur's court and preferred the historically oriented tale of a fine leader whose charisma attracted the best of the minds and hearts of his time. So please note that this is all Jane Yolen's fault. She *asked* me to write an Arthurian-based story for young adults.

And a story sprang to mind almost instantly. That doesn't happen often.

You see, I had always been fascinated by a chapter in Rosemary Sutcliff's magnificent *Sword at Sunset*, and *that* was the story I wanted to tell—how King Arthur got horses large enough for his brave knights to ride. Not the usual Arthurian theme, to be sure.

And Jane compounded her involvement by making me revise and refine, suggesting all these "minor" changes that became major improvements in my yarn. I wish to acknowledge a severe indebtedness to Jane Yolen and to her assistant, Karen Weller-Watson.

I tip my hat to Richard Woods, O.P., whose previous research on Arthur was invaluable in substantiating my own private theories. And to Michael Scott, who came to my rescue on some historical points that eluded me. Significant, too, is the contribution of Scott MacMillan, who called my attention to a book called *The Black Horses of England*, which dealt with the historical reverence for these animals, exhibited by the extraordinary number of taverns called the Black Horse that are *only* to be found in the path of Artos's marches to his twelve battles.

I will also thank Simon Good, of the Good Company, for patiently driving me about Exeter and Topsham so I could get a feel for the terrain. It was he who made the most felicitous discovery: that the area above the port of Topsham was called Black Horse, surely a reference to the brief residence of Lord Artos's imported Libyans.

In writing this book, I have used a combination of Latin and Celtic names that would have been current in this period of time, when the tribes of fifth-century England were throwing off the last vestiges of Roman domination. It is also a means of distancing myself and my readers from the glamorous Hollywoodisms.

Farriery—or the craft of shoeing horses—is aligned with my own keen interest in all things equine. Let me give most profound thanks to Joseph Tobin, Master Farrier and Associate of the Worshipful Company of Farriers, for his invaluable assistance in the technical aspects of this story. Although artifacts of the farrier's craft, being iron, seldom survive for us to examine, sufficient evidence proves that the shoeing of horses goes back a long way ... possibly as far back as the chariot horses of Mesopotamia. Certainly there were shod horses among the nomadic hordes of the Russian steppes. Their direct descendants practice that art much as their ancestors did: *No hoof, no horse.*

Anne McCaffrey
at Dragonhold-Underhill

CAST OF CHARACTERS

GALWYN GAIUS VARIANUS, a Roman Celt; son of
    Decitus Varianus, a factor

ARTOS, *Comes Britannorum* (Count of Briton), also a
    Roman Celt

BERICUS   ⎱ two of Artos's Companions on the
BWLCH   ⎰   voyage

GRALIOR, captain of the *Corellia*; Galwyn's uncle by
    marriage

DECITUS VARIANUS, Galwyn's dead father

PRINCE CADOR OF DUMNONIA (Devon–Cornwall)

ERCUS, landlord at Burtigala

BALDUS AFRITUS, horse trader at Burtigala

TEGIDUS, merchant at Burtigala

PAPHNUTIUS, Egyptian horse trader at Septimania

NICETUS THE ELDER, horse trader

DOLCENUS, port officer at Isca

CANYD BAWN, horse-wise herbalist at Artos's Devan
    farm

ISWY, Cornovian rider
DECIUS GALLICANUS, rider
EGDYL THE WHITE, rider
NESTOR from Deva
YAYIN from Deva
DONAN from Deva
TELDYS, farm manager
DAPHNE, his wife
ALUN, smith at Deva
RATAN, apprentice smith
MANOB, sergeant of the troop
FIRKIN, rider at Deva
SOLVIN, hostler at Galwyn's father's estate
RHODRI, Canyd's brother and a horse trainer
SERENA, Galwyn's mother
FLORA and LAVINIA, his sisters
ODRAN, Galwyn's stepfather; combmaker
MELWAS, Flora's husband
GALLUS, Galwyn's infant nephew

CEI
GERAINT
GWALCHMEI
MEDRAUT } Artos's Companions at Camelot
DRUSTANUS
CYFWLCH
BEDWYR

ARLO, page at Camelot
EOAIN ALBIGENSIS, stable boy at Camelot

MASTER ILFOR, forge master and armorer at Camelot
MASTER GLEBUS, horse master
BORVO, apprentice smith
MAROS, apprentice smith
PRINCE MALDON, visitor at Camelot
SEXTUS TERTONIUS, armorer
PRINCE GENEIR
GREN, hostler of Prince Geneir

Horse and pony names:
SPADIX, bay pony bought by Galwyn
Libyan stallions: CORNIX, VICTOR, PAPHIN
Libyan mares (sixteen in all): SPLENDORA and
    DORCAS are the only ones named
RAVUS, gray stallion at Camelot

Historical personalities:
ARTOS (aka Arthur), the Bear, Comes Britannorum or
    Count of Britain, also *dux bellorum* (war leader)
AURELIUS AMBROSIUS, war leader with Vortigern
VORTIGERN, prince who united northern tribes
AELLE, Saxon King in Eburacom (York)
CADOR, Prince of Dumnonia
NENNIUS, monk chronicler
SAINT GERMANUS, monk chronicler
GILDAS, monk historian
KING MARK, King of Cornwall

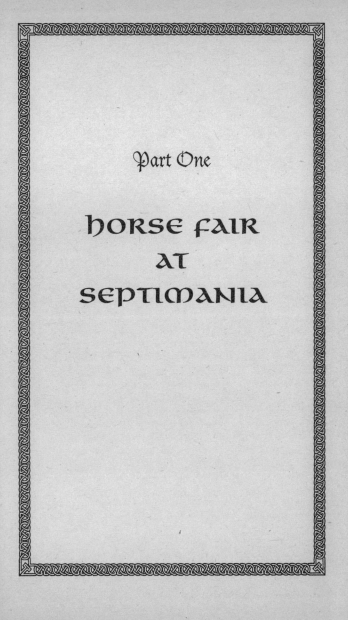

Part One

HORSE FAIR
AT
SEPTIMANIA

"GALWYN'S FEEDING the fishes again," the mate called as I emptied the odorous bucket overboard. I ignored him, rinsing the bucket in the strong waves that were following us from Isca Dumnorium.

By now, I was some used to crossing the Narrow Sea, but to have to tend to six grown men who were not, made me as ill as they. And made me, once again, the butt of jokes for my uncle's crew. It had taken me a while to learn not to rise to the mate's lures; he'd leave off his taunts sooner. "Have ye no sea blood in ye at all? Ye're no use in the rigging, little use on deck, and ye can't even keep b'low decks clean."

I was hauling the bucket up, had it nearly to the rail, when a particularly hungry wave caught and filled it. The line pulled burningly through my hands. I barely managed to belay it on a pin and thus not lose it entirely. The mate roared with laughter at my unhandiness, encouraging the other men of his watch to join him.

"Galwyn, I'd want proof that y'are indeed Gralior's nephew if I'd one like ye on any ship of mine."

3

The bucket forgotten, I whirled on him for that insult to my mother.

"Ah, lad, we've sore need of the bucket below," said a deep voice in my ear. A hand caught my shoulder with a powerful shake to gain my attention and curb my intent. "Such taunts are the currency of the petty," our noble passenger continued for my ear alone. "Treat them with the contempt they deserve." Then he went on in a tone meant to carry, "I tried the salted beef as you suggested, and it has succeeded in settling my belly. For which I'm obliged to you. I'll have another plate for my Companions."

I could not recall the *Comes*'s name—a Roman one, for all he was supposed to be as much of a Briton as the rest of us. My uncle treated him with more respect, even reverence, then he accorded most men, fare-paying passengers or not. So I was quite as willing to obey this Briton lord without quibble, and to ease his Companions' distress in any way I could. I hauled up the bucket, which he took below with him. Then I got more salt beef from the barrel before I followed him back down into the space assigned the passengers.

Warriors they might be, but on the sea and three days from land, they were in woeful condition: Two were green under their weathered skins, as they lay defeated by the roll and heave of the deck beneath them. I did not laugh, all too familiar with their malaise. They were big men, strong of arm and thew, with callused hands and arms scarred by swordplay. They'd swords in their baggage, and oiled leather jerkins well studded with nails. Big men in search of big horses to carry them into battle against the Saxons.

That much I had gleaned from snatches of their conversation before the seasickness robbed them of talk and dignity. Then they clung to their crosses and made soft prayers to God for deliverance.

"Come now, Bwlch, you see me revived," the war chief cajoled. Bwlch merely moaned as the salt beef was dangled in front of his face and gestured urgently to me to bring the bucket. There could be nothing now but bile in the man's stomach, if that, for he had drunk no more than a sip or two of water all day. "Bericus, will you not try young Galwyn's magic cure?" The second man-at-arms closed his eyes and slapped a great fist across his nose and mouth. "Come now, Companions, we are all but there, are we not, young Galwyn?"

I was mortified that he had remembered my name when I could not recall his and started to duck my head away from his smiling face. Now I was caught by the brilliant blue of his eyes and held by an indefinable link that made of me, in that one moment, his fervent adherent. Ah, if only my uncle had awarded me such a glance, I could have found my apprenticeship far easier to bear.

"Aye, sir," I said with an encouraging smile for the low-laid Bericus, "we'll make port soon, and that's the truth!" For landfall was indeed nigh. I'd seen the smudge on the horizon when I emptied the bucket, though the mate's taunt had driven the fact out of my mind till now. "We should be up the river to Burtigala by dusk. Solid, dry land."

"Artos, if the rest of this mad scheme of yours is as perilous as this . . ." Bericus said in a petulant growl.

"Come now, *amicus*," their leader replied cheerfully, "this very evening I shall see you served meat, fowl, fish, whatever viand you wish . . ." Each suggestion brought a groan from Bericus, and Bwlch tossed his soiled mantle over his head.

"We're in the river now, lord," I said to the *Comes Britannorum* Artos—for his full style came back to me now. I could feel the difference in the ship's motion. "If you'd come up on deck now, sirs, you'll not find the motion so distressing as lying athwart it down here."

Lord Artos flashed me a grin and, hauling the reluctant Bericus to his feet, said, "That's a good thought, lad. Come, clear your heads of the sick miasma. Fresh air is what you need now to set you right." He gestured for me to help Bwlch as he went to rouse the rest of his Companions.

They staggered onto deck, almost falling back down the ladder at the impact of the cool air. One and all, they reeled across, with me hard put to get them to the leeward rail, lest they find their own spew whipped back into their faces.

"Look at the land," I suggested. "Not the sea, nor the deck. The land won't move."

"If it does, I shall never be the same," Bericus muttered with a dark glance toward his leader, who stood, feet braced, head up, his long tawny hair whipping in the wind like a legion pennant. Bericus groaned. "And to think we've got to come back this same way!"

"It will not be as bad on the way home, sir," I said to encourage him.

He raised his eyebrows, his pale eyes bright in amazement. "Nay, it'll be worse, for we'll have the bloody horses to tend . . . on that!" He gestured behind him at the following seas. "Bwlch, d'you know? Can horses get seasick?"

"I'll be sure to purchase only those guaranteed to have sea legs," the *Comes* said with a wink to me.

I looked away lest any of the others misconstrue my expression. For this was August, and the crossing had been reasonably calm. In a month or so the autumn gales could start, and those could be turbulent enough to empty the bellies of hardened seamen.

"Have you far to travel on land?" I asked.

"To the horse fair at Septimania," Lord Artos said negligently.

"Where might that be, lord?"

His eyes twinkled approval at my question. "In the shadow of the Pyrenaei Mountains, in Narbo Martius."

"That far, lord?" I was aghast.

"To find that which I must have"—and his voice altered, his eyes lost their focus, and his fists clenched above the railing—"to do what I must do . . ."

I felt a surge run up from my bowels at the stern purpose of his manner and experienced an errant desire to smooth his way however I could. Foolish of me, who had so little to offer anyone. And yet this Britic war chief was a man above men. I did not know why, but he made me, an insignificant and inept apprentice, feel less a failure and more confident.

"And it is mine to do," he added, exhaling gustily. Then he smiled down at me, allowing me a small share of his certain goal.

"I need big strong mares and stallions to breed the warhorses we need to drive the Saxons out of our lands and back into the sea," he went on. "Horses powerful enough to carry warriors in full regalia, fast and far. For it is the swift, unexpected strike that will cause havoc among the Saxon forces, unaccustomed as they are to cavalry in battle. Julius Caesar used the *alauda*, his Germanic cavalry, to good effect against the Gauls. I shall take that page from the scroll of his accomplishments and protect Britain with *my* horsemen. If God is with us, the mares and stallions I need will be at that horse fair in Septimania, bred by the Goths from the same Libyan blood stock that the Romans used."

"Will not the legions return, lord, to help us?" I asked hopefully.

Lord Artos gave me a kind smile. "No, lad, we cannot expect them. This we must do for ourselves. The horses are the key."

"*Do* horses get seasick?" Bericus asked again, this time pointedly.

"The legions got theirs to Britain. Why can we not do the same?" the *Comes* asked with a wry grin.

"But how, lord, will you transport them?" And I gestured at the narrow hatch to the lower deck. Not even a shaggy Sorviodunum pony could pass through it.

"Ah, now that's the easy part," Artos said, rubbing his big, scarred hands together. "Cador and I worked that out." My eyes must have bulged at his casual reference to our prince of Dumnonia, for he gave me another reassuring smile that somehow included me in such exalted company. "We lift the deck planks, settle the horses below in pens well bedded with straw, and nail the planks back on. Simple, *sa?*"

I was not the only dubious listener; Bericus shook

8

his head and Bwlch covered his mouth for a cough. But the Lord Artos seemed so sure, and Prince Cador had the reputation of a formidably acute man.

"How big are the horses from Septimania?" I asked.

Artos put his forearm at a level with his eyes. "That height in the shoulder."

I could only stare at him in amazement. "Surely horses are not meant to grow that big?"

"Whyever not, Galwyn? When *we* have"—and Artos gestured to his Companions, all of whom towered above me, though I was considered the tall one of my kin.

Then my uncle came on deck as the *Corellia* ran up the mouth of the broad Gallish river to the harbor at Burtigala as if eager to end her journey. I hoped that there would be a cargo for us to return with, or my uncle's humor would be sour indeed. On this outbound trip, there had only been a load of bullhides, though the seven passengers had been a godsend and made the sailing worthwhile.

"Bring down the mainsheet," shouted my uncle, and he grunted with approval as the mate sent a kick after one of the sailors who moved too slowly. "Stand by the anchor and the landing lines. Do you have to be told every time? You, boy, what are you staring at? Lend a hand. You'll never make a seaman at this rate!"

I raced to grab up the line, which I was expected to take with me when I jumped ashore to the wharf, to help secure the ship. In my mind, I rebelled at "making a seaman," even on a ship that had been bought by gold from my father, who was helping his wife's brother

9

up in the world: a fact I knew but was astute enough never to mention even if the knowledge galled me.

"Look lively, you lump of a lad," he shouted at me, though the wharf was still too far away for me to jump. I'd fallen into the cold waters of the harbor often enough not to wish to do so now in front of Lord Artos.

I'd never make a seaman, not the sort my uncle wanted. My real value to him, and the reason he had taken me on in the first place and tolerated my other shortcomings, was my skill with languages and my ability to translate some of the barbarous trading dialects. This fluency allowed me to help him find good cargoes, and thus maintain myself in his good graces.

From childhood, I had been exposed to many foreign tongues. My father, Decitus Varianus, had been a factor and met folk from as far away as Egypt and Greece to the east, and some of the roving Nordic folk from the north. An outgoing, curious child, I had picked up snitches and snatches of many languages—sometimes hardly knowing what I was saying—but the facility remained and was improved upon by tutors in Greek and Latin, the Gaelic of our hill farmers, and indeed, whatever outlandish speech was spoken around me.

"What are you waiting for, Galwyn?" my uncle yelled at me as the distance to the pier narrowed slowly. It was still too far away, and out of the corner of my eye, I saw Lord Artos extend a hand as if to stay me from jumping at that command. "Scared, are you? Son of a bankrupt, taken in by me out of kindness to my sister-in-law! Are you going to be as much a failure as your father? Spoiled you are, and I trying to make a man out of you. Jump, I say. Jump!"

The ship was close enough now and I gathered myself for the leap, although, once again, Lord Artos's hand lifted to forestall me. But I knew my own abilities, even with all my limitations being shouted out in a litany.

I landed safely, whipping the line around the bollard and securing it in the bowline as I had been taught. I was rather pleased with myself, actually, since the jump had been wider than usual. When I looked back to see if Lord Artos approved of my feat, my chest swelled a bit to see him nod. Then I noticed that both Bericus and Bwlch looked less wan and pale. The ship still rocked in the current, but the fact that they were securely fastened to dry land again must have nearly restored them.

There was the usual bustle at the pier, with hawkers trying to sell fresh food and wine, and others offering their services in unloading cargo. My uncle gave unnecessary orders in a loud voice to impress the landsmen, but he was in no hurry to off-load the bull-hides and show the *Corellia* to be carrying so little of value.

My main duty in landing done, I hovered around Lord Artos and his Companions, helping them with their packs and gear. I was unwilling to leave their company. Well, *his* company.

"Galwyn," my uncle bawled, "make yourself useful for once. Help the lords with their baggage. And lead them to the Golden Swan. It's the only place in the port that would suit friends of Prince Cador's. Go with them so the landlord knows he's to give them his best . . . Only thing you are good for," he went on, though not as loudly, "is cackling in whatever it is they speak here! How you know what's what from all that gabble, I wouldn't know." He shook his finger at me. "See that you listen well and make sure this *Comes* is well taken care of. You hear me, now, Galwyn."

"Yes, uncle . . . Of course, uncle . . . I understand, uncle," I said whenever I could insert a word. I tried not to give away how happy I was to carry out that order. It wouldn't suit Gralior to think he had me doing something I wanted to do.

Then my uncle, all obsequious, bowed Lord Artos and his Companions down the plank that served to connect ship to shore.

"The lad knows the way, Lord Artos, and the rough speech that's all the landlord of the Swan can manage. Not a civil word in that man's head, but Galwyn will let him know that he will have no more of my trade if he does not give you of his best." Then, almost snarling at me because Bericus, Bwlch, and the others were picking up their own travel gear—"Take the packs, Galwyn. Help them. Don't just stand there with both arms the same length. You're not a spoiled juvenile now. You *work* for your living."

Scooting out of the way of my uncle's heavy-sandaled foot, I tried to take one of the packs from Lord Artos, but his hand restrained me.

"Lead on, Galwyn, lad, there's a good fellow," the *Comes* said, and gave me a gentle push.

I caught one glimpse of Gralior scowling at me and

hoped that he would have recovered by the time I returned. *Perhaps*, I thought traitorously, *I can delay*.

"And come you right back, Galwyn. There's cargo to unload," my uncle shouted just as we reached the first dwellings.

WELL, THE GOLDEN SWAN was a distance from the harbor. Even my uncle had to admit that, and I could always say that it took me a while to get the landlord to understand exactly what was needed.

In truth, I knew the local dialect so well that I had no trouble at all making Landlord Ercus understand that these guests were men of quality and rank. Besides, any fool could have seen that in a glance, and Ercus was no fool.

"My uncle, the good Gralior," I began tactfully, "said that only your inn would serve the *Comes Britannorum* and his Companions. You do have rooms available?"

"Of a certainty I do, young Galwyn," Ercus said, for he could be as tactful as I. "And as good a meal as any could ask for after a sea voyage."

"Well, they do need your very best food to settle their stomachs, Ercus."

And I reported my conversation to Lord Artos, who smiled and nodded. Then I went to the business of settling a price for the lodgings and determining how long they would be needed.

"You are hosting friends of Prince Cador, who trades here often enough for you to give your best price to these," I said. It took me time enough to argue his price down, but I did it. Fortunately, Artos had gold

13

rings to pay for his needs and these were accepted everywhere.

"For the one room large enough to sleep the six of you, he will charge a quarter ring." I turned to Artos. "Another quarter to feed you, but the wine you drink is extra. He does have good wine," I added, for I knew Ercus's reputation from other inns.

So the prices were settled, and as a meal could be served immediately to the men made very hungry by the three days' abstinence, I had no choice but to leave them to it.

I trotted the last few streets so that I would arrive breathless at the ship and perhaps prove to my uncle that I had arranged matters with dispatch.

THAT NIGHT, AS I LAY on a straw pallet in the hold of the *Corellia*, which was still redolent of seasick odors, I thought of *Comes* Artos's quest. Horses! How much I missed our horses. Before my father had lost all his substance in two seasons of disastrous storms, we had had many fine beasts in our stables. I had owned a fine mettlesome pony whom I had ridden as if we two were a single centaur. My father's sergeant-at-arms had grudgingly admitted that I was likely to make a competent horseman, and that was praise indeed from that stern fellow. What time I had to spare from my lessons and duties as my father's heir had been spent in the stable.

I ought not even to have thought of horses; they brought back too many painful memories. But I could scarcely help myself. Fine big strong horses, to be ridden by fine big strong men! Surely they'd need a horse boy to assist them on their travels? Surely I could make myself so useful to the *Comes Britannorum* that he would beg the loan of me from my uncle. That faint hope blossomed into determination as I lay there listening to the creaks and groans of the ship, and the restless slap of the river against her hull.

There is little that travels faster in a seaport town than word of rich patrons and mad quests. But I only learned of the rumors later, for at first light my uncle had roused me to accompany him while he bargained for some suitable cargo. Local wine and oil in amphorae, several bales of fine Egyptian cotton cloth, and some beautifully tanned and colored Ibernian leather were acquired by midmorning, and my uncle was not displeased, though never so much as a word of thanks—much less praise—rewarded my efforts. In truth, I had had no trouble with the corrupt Latin, larded though it was with the wretched Ibernian patois.

I was back on board the *Corellia* when the stable lad of the inn came with a message for my uncle from Lord Artos. My uncle scowled as he scanned the scrap of parchment, and then he glanced ominously at me.

"Humph. He's asked for you, boy. Seems as if you did as you were told for once and saw them well settled at the Swan. Now he needs your tongue to buy mounts for his journey," my uncle said. "Off you go, and use your wits for Lord Artos's sake in this matter, too. Prince Cador would have him assisted in every way, even by such a one as you."

He gave me a light cuff to remind me of my manners, and I scrambled off the ship and after the inn lad as fast as I could—before the expression on my face could ruin this opportunity.

Not only did I know languages, I knew horses. Perhaps my notion of becoming indispensable to Lord Artos had some chance. My uncle had his cargo—with my help. Could I not now become part of this quest for great warrior horses?

THE *Comes* AND HIS COMPANIONS had slept late, despite the noise about the busy inn, and had just finished breaking their fast when I rushed in upon them.

"*Ave*, Galwyn, well come," Artos said, expansively gesturing me to their table. It bore little but crumbs, and so many empty platters that I suspected his Companions had made up for the three days of meals they'd missed. Lord Artos caught my glance and his grin was mischievous. "I haven't understood a word that's been said to us. This Ercus, our host, garbles Latin as if he's chewing tough beef. Signs suffice in ordering a meal, but I'd rather know the price I must pay for decent mounts and to hire a reliable caravan leader."

"It's my honor, Lord Artos, my honor," I managed to reply, curbing an impulse to puff my experience in such matters. I would prove it with deeds, not words.

ONCE AWAY FROM THE PORT, Burtigala spread out, sprawling beyond the town boundaries originally set up by the Roman governors of the province. The bustling market area was built on the Roman design, despite the cramped tiny stalls that cluttered the space near the slave pens and along the animal fields. There were many people about, and I noticed the Companions staring at the occasional Nubian, black and splendid in richly colored robes; the slim, swart men whose rolling gait marked them as traders from the Levant; the big Goths swaggering an arrogant path through the crowds of small-statured folk. All, in their turn, marked my Lord Artos and his tall, muscular Companions and slowed their pace so that they did not overrun us. All around were the jabbering and liquid sounds of many languages, fragments of which I could identify as we passed the speakers.

"Is it always like this, Galwyn?" Bericus asked out of the side of his mouth.

"It is, sir; only sometimes much more so."

"More so?" Bwlch asked.

"This is not a market day, sir. Or a feast day."

"God has been good?" Bwlch muttered under his breath.

As soon as we reached the animal market, Baldus Afritus pushed his way forward to meet us, his sizable paunch clearing his path. He wore his oily smile and smoothed his soiled robes over his belly. I murmured a *caveat emptor* to Lord Artos. "Do not overtrust this one, *Comes*."

"Baldus Afritus at your service, noble lord," the man said unctuously in his heavily accented Latin, giving a Legion salute that Lord Artos ignored. Baldus now repeated his introduction in an even more garbled Gallic.

"Mounts," Lord Artos answered in Latin, moving to the rails, where he cast his eyes over the rugged ponies displayed. "Seven to ride, of at least fourteen hands of height, and four pack animals."

The smile on Baldus's face increased as he saw a fat profit for the day. "I have many fine strong ponies that would carry you from here to Rome with no trouble."

I snickered. Most of Baldus's "fine strong ponies" had no flesh on their bones, even this late into a fine summer. Their hooves were untrimmed, their backs scabby with rain rash, and their withers white with old sores from badly fitting pack saddles. And the majority were so small that Lord Artos's tall men would have to ride with their knees up under their chins.

"And what do you think of Baldus's offerings?" Lord Artos asked me, his eyes slightly narrowed as he gazed at me. Baldus watched me, too.

So, as if we were discussing the weather and not the beasts, I gave the lord my assessment, speaking in our own dear language, of which Baldus knew little.

"Not one that would last the trip?" Artos went on.

"Two only, lord, the bay with the star and snip, and the brown horse with the white sock on the off-hind."

Lord Artos gave a nod and walked on—despite Baldus's protestations—to the next pen, which, in truth, contained animals in little better shape. I could almost feel Baldus's stare piercing my shoulder blades.

In that lot, a second sturdy brown looked up to bearing the weight of one of the Companions as it dozed, hip-shot in the sun.

BY THE END OF THE DAY, after much looking and then considerable checking of teeth and tendons, backs, and wind—with either Bericus, Bwlch, or me backing a full dozen to judge their paces—Lord Artos struck a bargain for four. Baldus and another coper vied with each other, promising that more beautiful, stronger animals would be brought up from lush pastures farther from Burtigala so that the noble lords would have the most suitable beasts available. I was sent off to arrange for grain, a separate field to keep them in, a trustworthy lad to watch them, and a man capable of trimming their hooves for the journey.

"You've a keen eye, lad," Lord Artos said, laying a friendly arm across my shoulders as he and the Companions made their way back to the inn, "a light hand and a good seat. You're better riding the horses of the land than those of the sea, aren't you?"

I could only nod, overwhelmed with delight at his praise.

He clapped me companionably. "Will your uncle indulge me with your services for tomorrow as well? That is, after you've ordered a proper meal from our barbarian landlord."

THAT EVENING, TO MY SURPRISE and relief—for I had been having a sorry time of it loading cargo with the crew—Bericus came clattering down to the docks, leading one of the ponies purchased that morning.

"There's a merchant, an honest man by the look of him," Bericus said after a courteous greeting to my uncle. "But Lord Artos can make nothing of his speech. May we have the good offices of young Galwyn? My lord would deem it a great favor."

It was deftly done, for I saw Bericus slip something into my uncle's palm, which caused him to smile broadly and summarily gesture me to attend the Companion.

I was filthy, my cheek bloodied from a crate that happened to slip, and limping from another that had been purposely dumped on my foot.

"I cannot go to Lord Artos like this," I said, mortified at my state.

"The *Comes* cannot wait on you!" my uncle said, and before I realized his intent, he pitched me over the side of the ship. "You'll be clean enough when you've dried off," he bellowed down at me.

"Why, you sodden son of Mithras," Bericus yelled fiercely, "the lad's needed sound, not drowned!"

I had been in no danger, since I could swim well, and I was pleased that Bericus had rounded on my uncle for his treatment of me. I was even more grateful when Bericus hauled me up out of the water.

"Does he treat you often thus?" Bericus asked in a disgusted undertone.

"I *am* cleaner," I said ruefully.

Bericus grunted as he lifted a piece of seaweed from my shoulder and deposited it back in the harbor.

"The evening's warm enough that you should dry out on the ride back. Your tunic is certainly thin enough," Bericus added, and shot one more fierce glance at my uncle, whose back was to us.

We mounted, and the pony's warm back took some of the chill of the harbor water out of me.

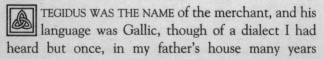 TEGIDUS WAS THE NAME of the merchant, and his language was Gallic, though of a dialect I had heard but once, in my father's house many years

before. He, too, wished to buy horses at Septimania, though his search was not for the same breed as ours.

"Ours," indeed! How brash I was!

He had trade to exchange as well, and he had worried about arriving safely in Septimania until he heard of the *Comes* Artos and his Companions, such obviously valiant warriors. He had come as far as Burtigala by ship, in a fair-sized party, and he hoped that if the Companions joined him he could start the long journey in two days' time. They had but to finish buying mounts and pack animals, as they had brought their own supplies.

"I believe the man," Lord Artos said, smoothing his beard around his smile. "What is your opinion, young Galwyn?"

"Mine, sir?"

"Do you think him honest?"

"He is who he says he is, Lord Artos, for my father had dealings with him many years ago. I remember the name, and that the dealings were well conducted."

"Tell Tegidus that we would be glad to join him and his band, and we will set out tomorrow as soon as we have mounts."

"My lord, we could go now to the farm and buy the ponies before Baldus gets them and doubles the price, as he will if he knows there is a demand."

Lord Artos peered at the darkening sky. "Is there time?"

"Enough if you ride now!"

The twinkle returned to the *Comes*'s eyes, and his beard framed a wide smile. "Inform Tegidus of your suggestion. We can offer him a mount to accompany us."

Bericus procured torches from the landlord, and the four of us were mounted and riding down the road in less time than it takes to tell it. We roused the herder from a bed he was loath to leave; he stood in the doorway, scratching himself.

"I've an early start in the morning to the market at Burtigala," he whinged, but brightened when he heard Tegidus clink his bag of coin.

"Perhaps we can save you that long journey and provide more profit than you would realize from Baldus," I said, winking.

"Ah, that one! Skin you of your hide and sell your meat for beef, he would!"

Granted, it is not generally advisable to buy ponies in the dark, but knowing hands can find curb and splint, and check hoof, tooth, and condition. These were sturdy mountain stock with flesh on their bones, hard hooves, and good frogs, and young enough to be easily resold on return. They were sure of foot, too, for which I was thankful as Bericus and I raced them up and down the hill to test their wind.

Before the glass could be turned for the new day, we left the farm, each leading four well-grown ponies. My arms were nearly pulled out of their sockets by the time we reached Burtigala, my legs ached with the strain of holding me on the withers of my own mount, and my thighs were chafed from the rough saddle pad.

"How is that you speak my tongue so well?" Tegidus asked me as we turned the animals out in the rented paddock.

"I saw you in the house of my father."

"Did you? And he was . . ."

"Decitus Varianus," I said, although my throat went tight in memory of my father and those happier days.

"Ah! You're the little lad who chirped so happily in any language he heard." Tegidus's white-toothed smile was briefly illuminated by the sputtering torches. "I was sorry to hear of your father's death, lad. You are well employed with Lord Artos, but you have been more than helpful to an old friend this day." He tucked something in my hand that I, in turn, lodged in my belt, too weary to dispute the unnecessary vail or set his notion of my employment to rights.

I DO NOT RECALL HOW, but I seem to have spent the night in Lord Artos's chamber, on a pallet by the foot of the bed he shared with Bwlch and Bericus.

Knowing that the loading of my uncle's ship continued that morning, I was somewhat concerned for my absence.

"Nonsense, lad," Lord Artos said. "Bwlch will return with you to spare you reproaches, but you have been of invaluable assistance to me, which is as Prince Cador charged your uncle. You have done no wrong."

When Bwlch and I reached the ship, the crew were already busy hauling bales and amphorae up the gangplank. My uncle's expression when he saw me gave me pause, though it turned courteous enough when he bowed and smiled at Bwlch.

"You have our thanks, lad," Bwlch said loudly as I handed over the reins of the pony I had ridden. As he took the lead from me, he pressed some coins in my hand, grinned, and winked, then clattered off, his long legs dangling almost to his mount's knees.

Hastily I concealed the coins in my belt. Just in time, too, for my uncle was hauling me by the ear back up the plank, cursing under his breath.

"Your fine friends are gone now, lad, and you'll do the work you were hired for."

I do not know what put my uncle in such a bad mood, for I *had* done the work I was hired for, in dealing for the cargo. Yet I still had to help load. It was a weary, weary day, with cuffs and blows and kicks to speed me at tasks. I did my best, but sometimes it seemed they left the most unwieldy lots for me, heavy beyond my strength; and then they laughed as I strained and heaved with little avail. I paid dearly that day for those hours with Lord Artos.

I would have paid twice the price, had it been asked.

I WAS SO EXHAUSTED by nightfall that I could not summon the energy to eat. Instead I crept into a space between deck and cargo where few could find me. In the dark, I transferred the coins and the gold ring Tegidus had given me into my worn empty pouch and tucked all safely back under my belt. As soon as I laid my head down, I was asleep.

The cold roused me, even buffered as I was between bundles and deck. The clammy sort of cold that suggests a dense fog. Groaning, I realized that my uncle's humor—for he had planned to sail with the morning tide—would scarcely improve. I could not stay hidden all day, however preferable that would be. When I heard the others stirring and grumbling at the weather, I crept out, shivering. Hunger drove me to the galley, and though I did manage to snatch a heel of bread, the cook put me to work immediately. I was struggling with a sack of the beans he intended to soak for the evening meal when the little pouch fell from my belt.

The first mate saw it and snatched it up. "Ah, what have we here? Light-fingered is he, too, this bastard scum of a Cornovian?"

I do not know what prompted me, save that I had had enough of him and of my miserable existence on the *Corellia*, with only the prospect of more of the same until my spirit was completely broken.

Because he held the pouch aloft, dangling from the drawstrings, I saw my chance. I leapt, catching the pouch; and in another leap, dove over the side of the ship, swimming through the still water and losing myself in the mist. Even the shouts and curses from shipboard were quickly muffled in that thick fog.

When my first frantic strokes exhausted me, I tread the water, terrified that perhaps I had swum in the wrong direction. Some early-morning garbage bobbed about me, and listening avidly, I heard the unmistakable lap of water against a shore. I struck out toward the sound.

At last I hauled myself out, gasping for breath and shivering in the raw air, but filled with a sort of triumph. I had escaped! I would join Lord Artos. Had he not said that I was useful to him with my gift of tongues? He would need someone to interpret Tegidus on the long road they would travel together. He would surely need my skills at Septimania.

I opened the purse to count my worldly wealth and found it far more than I had expected. Several small coins of the sort we use in Britain, and two, not one, gold rings of the sort that traders carry, current in any port. I could scarcely believe such good fortune and generosity. This should prove enough—for I knew how to haggle—to buy a warm cloak and leggings, as well as a pony from the farmer. I knew the one I wanted, too small for most men to ride but the right size for me.

None of the traders in the marketplace—all glad of any dealings on such a foggy morning—questioned my wealth or my reasons. I managed to buy some travel bread and grain.

BY THE TIME I REACHED the farm, the fog still held the coastline in its white roll. But the little bay pony I had noted grazed in the meadow. The farmer was in an expansive mood, having sold his best at a good profit to Tegidus and Lord Artos with no recourse to a villain like Baldus. He was quite willing to sell me the pony, for—as I was quick to point out—it was indeed too short in the leg to suit a man of any tribe. Out of kindness, he patched together a bridle of sorts and showed me how to wrap the folds of my cloak to make a pad.

"I shall call him Spadix," I told the farmer, naming the pony for his bay color.

"A good name," the farmer agreed.

I trotted off up the road, certain that Lord Artos would not be far ahead.

BY EVENING, when I had met few travelers, and none I liked the look of, I was having doubts about the whole venture. I ate my travel bread by a stream well off the track, then hobbled the pony in a fair patch of grass. Curling up in my cloak, I spent an uneasy night. The ground had this tendency to roll beneath me, and I kept waking in a fright that I was still aboard the *Corellia*.

IT TOOK ME THREE DAYS to catch up with Lord Artos's band. They were making camp and someone had hunted successfully, for a pot burbled with appetizing odors on a tripod over a good hot fire.

Tegidus saw me first, rushing up to me, gesticulating wildly, his expression both welcoming and anxious. "The oak has answered my prayers, young Varianus, for I should not have undertaken this journey so cheerfully if I had known you would not be among their number, to translate the gabble they speak."

"Lord Artos, it is Galwyn, come to rescue us from ignorance!" Bericus roared. Before I knew it, my pony and I were ringed with babbling men, pulling me one way or the other.

"Your uncle relented, then?" Lord Artos asked as he waded through the importunate crowd. He did not stop to hear what my answer might have been, and so I never had to give him a lie at all. "By God's eye, I'm glad enough to see you. Signs, signals, and smiles do not make good communications. You are well come, young Galwyn, well come indeed."

"He says that our animals are overloaded," Tegidus complained to me. "He will not let us cook a midday meal and insists that we all take a turn at watch at night. Watch at night? I? That is why we travel with him. So that he may guard."

"Those fools have packed their animals so badly

that half have sores," was Bericus's plaint, "and they will not attend when we show them how to rearrange the loads properly."

It took me only a few minutes to explain, each to the other, what was amiss, and to set it right.

Then to my everlasting joy, Lord Artos encircled my shoulder with his great arm and led me to their campfire. No matter if I was listed as a runaway apprentice by my spiteful uncle—I would gladly spend the rest of my life on a galley bench to have the mark of Lord Artos's favor now. Bwlch heaped me a huge plate of rabbit stew, which did much to quiet my stomach. And I did not have to stand watch or help the cooks—at least that first night.

THE JOURNEY TO SEPTIMANIA was not without its trials: Unusual icy storms in the mountains being the least of them, and steep and rough roads the worst. The best evenings were when we'd sit about the campfire, talking. It was then I learned more about my lord Artos's plans. I also relearned certain historical facts that I probably had had from my tutor but had forgotten—more likely ignored, as I had been an indifferent scholar. The *Comes* spoke of Aurelius Ambrosius, who had been his mentor—and incidentally, one of the heroes who had followed Vortigern when that prince had united the northern tribes to drive the Pict invaders back over Hadrian's Wall.

"Which is how the Saxons got invited into Britain," Lord Artos remarked with a rueful smile. "To help repel the Picts. Guests who have long outstayed their welcome."

His Companions nodded in solemn agreement.

"Why had Vortigern done that?" The question burst from me, usually silent while my betters spoke.

Lord Artos grimaced at me across the fire, his face taking on a gargoyle look in the flames. "We had no other choice," he said, and I knew then he spoke as *Comes Britannorum*, for he was not old enough to have been part of that victorious force. "The Roman legions that had guarded the Wall for so long had pulled out, and Rome itself did not answer our pleas for assistance." He shrugged. "We had to have reinforcements."

"Hallelujah!" Bericus said with a wicked smile. I later learned that "Hallelujah!" had been the battle cry that Saint Germanus taught Vortigern's troops. Many felt that it had helped Vortigern succeed against the Picts.

"If 'Hallelujah' *and* the big horses help us drive the Saxons back into the sea, I will shout it at the top of my lungs," Lord Artos said, and all about the fire added, "Amen!"

I said nothing then, mindful that Lord Artos and his Companions wore the crosses of the Christian ethic and spoke of God, rather than gods; and of this I was glad. My uncle and his crew were pagan in their superstitions and I had never had a chance to hear mass in my uncle's employ. At that, I was exceedingly grateful my uncle was not my blood kin, but my mother's younger sister's husband.

My mother had looked down on that marriage as beneath what her sister could have achieved. Only now did I realize that my mother had done very well indeed to have attracted the substantial man my Christian father had been. He had adored her and given her everything she desired. For the first time, I thought how bitter she must be about losing the lovely villa that had been our home, she herself driven off with my two sisters after his death, each carrying naught but shawl-wrapped bundles of personal belongings that would have brought my father's creditors little in their selling.

THE NEXT DAY we traversed the first of the rocky gorges on our way to Septimania. Keeping Spadix far from the edges of those sheer-sided drops, I prayed silently but with great vigor and enthusiasm. We lost one pack mule over the side; but while Tegidus mourned the loss of its burden, by the time we had crossed the last of the mountainous barriers to our destination, he was relieved that it had been the only casualty.

As we came down from those mountains, we could see the vast valley of Narbo Martius spread out, with the huge temporary town of the horse fair making brilliant-colored splotches with its tents—some even made of carpets from Arabia. We were two days early and used that time to settle in, camping apart from but near enough to Tegidus's site to continue the protection agreed upon.

I was sent with Bericus and Bwlch to find provisions from the stalls and tents of local vendors. A barbarous version of Latin was the main language, but I also heard, and stored, the camp jargon with which Latin was basely mixed. Some words and phrases I understood only from their context, but I was quick-minded enough to figure out what was meant.

Then, with Lord Artos and the others, we toured the animals on display: horses, mules, jennies, donkeys, and even a few of the grotesque parodies of horses that are called camels. One spat a green and slimy mass at me—which required me to wash all my clothing in the river. I was careful not to come close enough to one of those beasts again. The Companions were sympathetic, and they did not laugh at my misfortune, as my uncle's crew would have done. In fact, they took careful note not to suffer the same treatment.

But that was a small price for me to pay to see the display of horseflesh: the graceful Barbs with their dish faces and delicate ears that nearly met above their polls; the sturdy little steppe ponies; the small fine-boned animals who enlivened our afternoons with their races.

Bericus lost as much as Bwlch won in wagers on the races. Lord Artos merely enjoyed the sight.

We found the Libyans, finally, late on the second morning—fortunately, before the fair started. By then I had had a chance to become somewhat fluent in the camp jargon and could recognize the words in some of the atrociously accented Latin that was common. Indeed, by the end of the third day, having to translate all sorts of languages and bad accents, my head ached from the effort of concentrating.

Still, the *Comes Britannorum* had a way with him in dealing with anyone, trader or prince, that seemed to compel respect and foster truth and honesty. He spoke to many, and others sought him out. And really, he was easy to find, for he and his Companions towered over all but the burly blond Goths.

There were displays of the horses, showing their paces, their skills, even jumping rough barriers to prove their agility. I marveled at the riders, usually slim wiry lads who stayed on the backs of fractious horses that reared and bucked and cast figures above ground as if the riders had been impaled astride. It was glorious and I was all but glutted by so many beautiful horses.

However, I did remember my duty to Lord Artos, and I discovered which one of the many traders could be trusted to sell us horses that were sound, free of vice, and unimpaired by those covert tricks by which clever traders hide defects. The man was an Egyptian, Paphnutius by name, and he was both gratified and pleased that he was the one Lord Artos decided to approach.

Paphnutius was of middle years, with piercing dark eyes and the most astounding hawk's nose on his thin swarthy face. He exuded a courtesy that others lacked.

"Come, *effendi*," he said, for his Latin was fluent if oddly accented. "Come into my humble tent and we will refresh ourselves. A man must have time to see and to reflect before any business." And he shrugged one shoulder to indicate that *business* was not as important as courtesy.

The Egyptian's tent was far more sumptuous inside than its exterior suggested.

"Sit, sit, do. Be comfortable," he said, with bows and sweeping gestures of his hand as he pointed to the thick cushions piled upon marvelous carpets. They glowed red and blue in a chamber lit by hanging lamps, which burned a scented oil. Then he clapped his hands. A woman—swathed all in black, so that only her eyes were visible—appeared at that summons; he gave her a curt order in his own language. It was too quick for me to be sure what he said, but I think it dealt with something to drink.

"You are from afar?" Paphnutius asked courteously, when we were all seated. I felt uncomfortable until I imitated his cross-legged posture.

"We are," Lord Artos said, looking amazingly dignified upon his cushion. "From Britain."

"Ah!" and Paphnutius's eyes went round with pleasure at such a revelation. "You have journeyed far indeed to see our poor horses."

Bericus gave a snort, because it was obvious to us all that the horses were far from poor.

Just then the woman returned with a beautiful brass tray and served us a thick, sweet beverage in tiny cups. One almost had to spoon it into the mouth, but this was evidently part of a bargaining ritual, similar to some I had seen my father perform with alien traders. I could almost think myself a child—and carefree—again in such an atmosphere.

"May I ask what this is we are drinking?" Lord Artos said, his tone one of surprised pleasure.

"It is called *qahwa*, and comes from a bean that is ground and then diffused in boiling water. The taste pleases the *effendi*?" Paphnutius was all concern that the drink might not please us.

I found it odd but certainly tasty: better than small beer or watered wine.

"It pleases me greatly," Lord Artos said, and paused to take another sip, smiling broadly. I caught him glancing about us to be sure we were also displaying pleasure. Which we all were. Odd the drink was, but I liked it.

Just then the woman reappeared, and this time her tray contained dates, pieces of ewe's cheese, and other sweet-tasting small cubes that were unknown to me.

"Was your journey arduous?" asked Paphnutius; and so we discussed that topic, and then the weather, and the situation of the camp, and only finally the vast number of horses that were on display.

At that point, Lord Artos rightly judged that business could be discussed, and with the sort of gracious reluctance that dealing with the Egyptian required, he explained his requirements. The mares should be proven fertile, preferably already in foal to Libyan stallions, and the stallions should be no more than four years of age and of proven virility. All the horses should be broken to saddle and bridle.

Paphnutius never asked *why* such breeding horses would be required by this foreign lord. Perhaps he could understand without explanation. After all, Lord Artos and all his companions were tall men; clearly they would need large mounts.

When we had finished our pleasant repast, Paphnutius guided us outside again and, clapping his hands, began the parade of the horses he had for sale.

"The mare is but four years old, and as you see by the foal at foot, she is fertile. This is her second foal." Then, from a parchment scroll he produced from somewhere in his voluminous robes, he rattled off a long pedigree that seemed to deal more with the performance of the dams than the sires. "She is in foal again, to the same sire."

This mare was big, wide hipped; and the foal at her foot was certainly five months old, for he had lost his fuzzy foal coat and was strong and lively. And nearly black. Both animals had good conformation and a fine sheen to their hides.

Paphnutius then gave us the stallion's pedigree, speaking as fast as he could for some time.

"Is he among those you have for sale?"

"Oh, no," and Paphnutius looked almost shocked. "He is renowned for his speed, and much in demand."

Lord Artos nudged me briefly as the mare and her energetic foal were taken back to the picket line.

"When will she foal, Paphnutius?" he asked as he watched her movements.

"In your springtime. I have the date . . ." And he consulted his parchment roll. "Ah, yes, she was covered in the third month and then confirmed in foal. Yes, yes, she is a fine mare to breed from." He looked a little wistful and I wondered why. I didn't know then that the Egyptians and Arabs preferred mares to stallions.

On the other hand, Bwlch looked concerned.

"What's wrong?" I asked discreetly, in our own tongue, lowering my voice so that the Egyptian didn't hear us.

"Spring at Deva, where Artos plans to send the horses, can be a cruelly cold season. We breed so that the mares will have their foals in late spring. The later the better. At least that one is well enough in foal so she'll be all right on the sea journey." Bwlch shook his head, already worried about that leg of the way back to Deva.

The parade of mares, some with foals at foot and others guaranteed in foal, continued. I tried to figure out which ones met with Lord Artos's approval; his expression remained the same, pleasant, smiling, outwardly favorable, throughout the entire display.

The stallions were shown next, and worked in circles on long lines to show their proud paces. The second one, not much taller than the first, displayed himself with just that little extra flick of his feet, a prouder carriage of his head and tail, an assurance that caught the eye, and a blue gleam to his silky black hide.

"Now, that's just the one for me," Lord Artos murmured to Bericus, although he kept his expression bland. "I would name him Cornix."

"What else, Artos!" Bericus whispered back, and winked at me. *Cornix* means "raven." I did not then know that ravens are the birds of good omen for the *Comes Britannorum*.

Paphnutius had nine stallions, more than were needed; but not all measured up to the criteria in Lord Artos's mind. Finally the parade ended, and then Lord Artos singled out his choices of mare and stallion. I missed out on only one mare and one stallion in my private selection.

"Ah, but come into my humble abode, Lord Artos," Paphnutius said then, bowing and scraping as he led the way, "for you must surely be thirsty. And one cannot discuss matters of such importance out here, where there are so many distractions."

So we retired again. More of the thick sweet *qahwa*

did indeed moisten a throat made dry by the dust the parade of horses had swirled up around us. I did justice to the sweetmeats, too, and more exotic ingredients were served this time. I don't remember half of the subtle combinations that passed into my mouth and down my gullet, because I had to concentrate more on the nuances of bargaining.

Memory of my father's tactics returned to me, and if I say so myself—and Lord Artos was very kindly complimentary that evening—I did very well at this business. Better than I ever did for Uncle Gralior; beatings do not encourage as surely as praise. I also wanted to prove to Lord Artos how indispensable I could be. I did not aspire to become a Companion, for I was too young and would never be of that size, but surely I could serve my lord in many other ways that could further his ends. My instruction in the short Roman swords still favored by soldiers had ended with my father's death, but perhaps I could retrain and join Artos's cohort.

When the deals had been completed, Paphnutius himself took us to a compatriot, Nicetus the Elder, several tents away to secure the remaining few horses that were needed. And there, with appropriate ceremonies, viewings, and bargainings, the remaining Libyans were purchased.

I was so excited that I could not sleep that night. I kept creeping out of our shelter to see if the Libyans were still picketed. Bericus was on watch.

"We won't lose them, Galwyn," he reassured me, and pointed out his sentry companion on the other side of the line. "Get your rest. You've earned it."

THE NEXT DAY Lord Artos sold off the now-unneeded ponies, for he would mount his men on some of the new acquisitions and lead the others. Spadix was not among those sold, because, he said, "I have no right to dispose of Captain Gralior's property."

I contrived not to look in his direction at that. Spadix was not my uncle's but truly mine, bought with the gratuities I had earned. However, this was not the time to mention that fact. And there was another reason to keep my pony. Cornix was the most unbiddable of the stallions—so wild he had had to be roped, tied, and twitched before a round bit could be inserted between his snapping jaws and a stout bridle attached to his head. Yet he was unexpectedly calm in Spadix's company. The sight of that little bay imp, who could easily stand beneath the stallion—and did so during the worst of the rains—was as ludicrous as it was beneficial.

The big mare that I now bestrode was nowhere near as comfortable to sit on as my short-coupled pony, and she had a foal at foot besides. It was a well-grown colt of some seven months, and he would reach up to nip my legs or heels if he felt I was interfering with his feeding. His dam was so broad in the withers I could barely get my legs around her and felt split apart when she trotted. Whereas the mate and his crew would have laughed their sides sore to see me, the Companions' smiles were good natured and not at my expense.

The stallions took much handling and I was glad that I was relegated to riding the more placid tempered mares. The stallions needed the firm hand and strong legs of the Companions to keep them under control. Bwlch and Bericus were considerable horsemen, the other Companions hardly less so. But Lord Artos was their superior, sitting lightly balanced on Cornix's black back, swaying slightly from the hips while the stallion cavorted or reared or bucked as it shied at the slightest unusual object on the track. He was well named, for like the raven, he was often without a foot to the ground, half in flight from some imagined terror.

Sometimes I think we traveled farther sideways and backward than forward, and yet we made good time on the return trip. Perhaps because we knew the way now, and its various hazards, and so could avoid them.

Once again, it was the conversations of the evening and the singing that entranced me. Bericus had a good tenor voice. Often Lord Artos would ask him for a special melody or song. On board the *Corellia*, I had forgotten about the music we used to have; my father and mother had kept a sweet-voiced slave who played the lyre while we dined with guests. The work chanteys that Gralior's men had sung as they hauled up sail or worked the capstan bar were coarse and repetitive, not truly music to my ear.

One of the mares bruised her foot on the rough gravel of the next-to-last pass we had to traverse. We had to wait a day, standing her in the cold running water of a stream to ease the soreness.

We spent a lot of time hanging about watching her when all the other tasks an open-air camp requires were done.

"No hoof, no horse," Lord Artos said at one point,

grinning broadly at Bericus, who raised his eyes heavenward.

"Eh?" was Bwlch's only response to this cryptic remark.

"And what'll old Canyd say about these hooves, Artos?" Bericus asked.

"Oh, him?" And Bwlch dismissed the man with a wave of his hand. "He's not been on at you about those iron sandals of his, has he, Artos?"

"The subject comes up periodically," Lord Artos said. "We'll have to travel fast over all kinds of ground. I meant to ask Paphnutius if he knew anything about such devices."

"Too late now," Bwlch said philosophically. "Though I saw no horses at Septimania with rims."

"Rims?" I asked, curious. I had never heard of the term in connection with horses.

"Iron costs money," Lord Artos said with an indifferent shrug.

Then the companions who had been hunting for the evening meal returned, and I heard no more about such sandals.

BY THE NEXT DAY, the mare could walk out well enough for us to continue.

On a fine bright warm afternoon, we came down out of the hills on the track past the farm where I had bought Spadix, and we saw Burtigala Port in the distance. I could just make out the masts of ships at anchor, and suddenly dread returned to me: What would I do if I encountered my uncle?

My anxiety deepened as we came closer to the town.

Mounted as I was on the tall mare named Splendora, I could see over the heads of pedestrians, and I scanned the ships for the familiar lines of the *Corellia*. To my intense relief she was not in port.

Then there was the business of settling the horses for the night and taking up residence in the same inn that Lord Artos had patronized just weeks before. Again my talents as interpreter were needed to assure us of proper accommodations and a good evening meal. Landlord Ercus, undoubtedly remembering how well Lord Artos had treated him before, was all-obliging. I wanted to know but could not bring myself to ask the man if the *Corellia* had docked recently.

THE NEXT MORNING I was up at the crack of dawn, peering down through the mists that swirled up from the sea; but there were no new ships tied up at the dock. Somewhat heartened, I went to the field with grain to feed the horses before anyone else usurped the task. I had them all watered and fed before a sleepy Bericus arrived.

"Ho, Galwyn, you deserved to lie and get your growth sleep," he said, ruffling my hair. "You've no need to do more than your share of the work. Have you a mind to join us for mass?" he asked.

"Of course," I said with enthusiasm. In a town as large as Burtigala there would be a place for Christians to worship, but as long as I had been on board the *Corellia* I had never dared ask my uncle's permission to attend mass.

The church was small and dark, and the priest mumbled the Latin. I think he was somewhat nervous about having such fine lords in the congregation that morning. I had to keep reminding myself of my good fortune as I made the proper responses.

During the rest of the day I was too busy to worry about my uncle. Prince Cador had requisitioned two fat sloops in which the *Comes* could ship his all-important mares and stallions across the Narrow Sea. The ships awaited our arrival. Both were half again the size of the *Corellia*, far newer and better maintained. The sails were not patched, the lines looked fresh and showed no splicings, the paint on the hulls had recently been scrubbed, and there probably wasn't a barnacle anywhere underwater. Their masters had also, according to instructions from Prince Cador, made certain preparations for this special cargo. The deck planks had been removed above the cargo area, which was just deep enough to accommodate Cornix, the tallest of the Libyans, and wide enough for four or five horses. They would be loaded head to tail, side by side, so that each would be cushioned by its mates against the roll and yaw of a rough sea. The inside of the hull had been padded with straw-filled mattresses as another safeguard against injury. The horses at least would be spared the wind and weather on deck and, with any luck, arrive unscathed at their destination.

We had some time, I can tell you, getting the horses into this area. As the most placid of the five who were to be loaded in the first ship, Spadix was hoisted in first. During that operation, he whickered nervously, despite my shouts of encouragement from where I stood in the well of the ship.

"Easy, Spadix, that's fine, I'm here. You're not in

danger!" I shouted, though I felt that I was in some danger. If the belly sling slipped, then Spadix would come crashing down on me. Still I didn't let that concern color my voice as I kept reassuring him. As soon as I could reach, I got hold of one hind hoof, then quickly I transferred my grasp to his front legs, stroking them as he settled to the deck, wild eyed, ears pricked, and nostrils flaring in his panic.

"There, lad, that wasn't so bad, was it?" I said, stroking his sweaty neck and gentling him out of his fright.

"Let's not delay, shall we, Galwyn?" Lord Artos called down to me. "We've four more to get in there, and then five in the other ship before dark, you know."

Stepping lively then, I unfastened the sling from Spadix and gestured for it to be hoisted out and away, as I walked the shaky-legged pony to his place against the starboard side of the ship.

The foal came next, and it was paralyzed with fear, so stiff-legged I could barely coax it to walk off the sling. His dam followed, in haste to answer the frightened neighs of her foal. I tied her next to Spadix. The foal pushed in against her, urgently needing to suckle, and she became calmer, although she kept her head up and stared about, wide eyed.

Although the sides of the hold had been cushioned with straw-filled mattresses, the overwhelming odors in this part of the ship were a combination of sea, oil, and the tar with which the sides of the ship were caulked. Surely the mare had smelled much the same combination when she had been sailed across the

Middle Sea. And maybe that's what was causing her distress.

The second mare was loaded almost without incident, though she snorted with nervousness at her strange new stable. Then I heard a good deal of shouting from the wharf as loud directions were issued by Lord Artos, with Bwlch and Bericus adding suggestions as to how to load Cornix.

"Blindfold!" Lord Artos cried. "He won't fear what he can't see. Where's something to blindfold him? I don't care if it's your best tunic, it'll cover his eyes."

"Hobble his feet, or he'll kick the lad to death as soon as he feels solid ground."

"Solid ground?" That came from Bwlch with a loud bark of laughter. "What's solid about a deck?"

"Hold him!"

"Watch his teeth! We should have tied his mouth shut, too."

The men began hauling the stallion on board. Craning my neck, I could see his black bulk, blindfolded and leg-tied, swinging in over the deck. Fortunately he didn't squirm as the mare had, though his sweat dripped down on my head. The lead chain dangled and I positioned myself to grab it.

"Whatever you do, Galwyn, *don't* remove that blindfold," Lord Artos called over the side.

"What about the hobbles?" I got hold of the long lead and carefully backed away from where Cornix would settle. He was swinging in the hoist and his teeth were bared, nostrils flaring red.

"Rear ones, I guess," Lord Artos replied, though his tone was dubious.

I got those off as the stallion was still being lowered, and since he was not the brightest horse I had ever met, he didn't realize his hind feet were free. He was also so confused that I was able to push him against the port side of the ship where he was to be tied. But I guess I didn't tie him to the ring soon enough. Nor did the sailors manage to get the deck planks down before he realized what was happening. Even I could feel that subtle compression of air above me as the planks were slammed back over the opening. The hammering made him nervous and he flinched with every blow.

Then I thought that if he could see he was safe here and the blows were only noise, he might settle. I uncovered his eyes.

And let loose a maniac.

He took one look at the dark confines of his new quarters and reared. I dangled from the end of his lead chain like a rat in a fighting dog's jaws.

When he came down, I dragged the lead rope through the ring, but he reared once more just as the last spike was being driven into the overhead planks. It missed his poll, but the shock of the point touching his ear startled him motionless with fright and I was able to pull the tether tight so he could not rear again.

I was as trembling and sweaty as he was. But beside him, Spadix nickered, and that seemed to comfort him. I had also brought on board some fresh grass I had pulled on the way to the harbor. This I fed to all the animals, hoping to calm them. I thanked the good Lord that they immediately fell to munching contentedly.

With them quiet, I could hear the muted shoutings

as the Companions loaded the other ship with its five equine passengers. It seemed to take such a long time. Finally, I heard feet running along the deck above me and again had to soothe the horses, though I had run out of the fresh grass by then.

At length I felt the unmistakable surge of the ship getting under way and knew that this leg of our journey had begun.

WE DISCOVERED, in the worst way possible, that horses can get seasick, though not as humans do. The stallion covered me with his scourings, though my Spadix—eyes white with fear, all four legs poking out stiffly—did not succumb. Yet it was not a rough crossing by my standards, and both ships stayed within sight of each other the entire way.

Bericus and Bwlch, who sailed in the same ship with me, were rather heartened that they were not affected by the sea motion on this return voyage. Truth to tell, we were all so busy with the horses, soothing them, cleaning up after them, coaxing them to eat the fragrant hay, that we humans simply had no time to be sick.

Lord Artos inspected the horses morning, noon, and night, and had himself rowed across to the second ship to perform the same offices as soon as he was done on ours. Never was I more relieved to see the mouth of the river on the horizon that afternoon. The Exe led to the port just above Isca.

"You'll be on land before dark, my lad," I murmured to the stallion. He stood with his head bowed between his splayed front legs, his finely shaped ears drooping to either side of his elegant head, his black coat grimed and rough with sweat though we had groomed him morning and night. Remembering his fine displays on land, it was disheartening to see his proud spirit so low. But then his head lifted suddenly and his nostrils flared as he smelled land.

I could have wished his spirits had taken slightly longer to revive, for he proved his old self when the deck planks were removed and he could see daylight. He trumpeted like a wild thing, pawing and thrashing at his tethers. I had to use my own tunic to cover his eyes while the pony was hoisted ashore first. Then it was the stallion's turn, and finally the two mares' and the foal's.

Cornix was weak, though, from the journey, and had trouble keeping his legs under him. There was an apprehensive look on his face as he staggered first this way and that, recovering land legs.

"*Ave, Comes Artos,*" cried a glad voice, and Prince Cador himself came riding down to the dock, more men behind him. "Magnificent, *Comes Britannorum!*" he exclaimed as he dismounted, throwing his reins to an aide. Appraisingly, he circled the stallion, his face expressing his high opinion. "Truly magnificent. Sixteen hands high if he's one!"

"Seventeen is more like it, Cador," Lord Artos said proudly. "Look at the bone of him, the breadth of his barrel, the power in his haunches. Oh, he's gaunt enough from three days at sea, but we'll put condition on him soon enough once he's at Deva. I have called him Cornix."

"Appropriate enough for you, my friend," Cador said

with a grin, glancing heavenward as if to see if any ravens were among the birds circling above. Then the prince turned to watch the first of the mares to be offloaded. "By Epona, the mares're up to his quality as well!" His bright light eyes widened as the mare swayed on feet made unsteady by her days at sea.

Bericus was at her side, giving her sufficient mass to lean against while she scattered her front legs. Then she whinnied wildly for her foal, who was already thrashing about in the hoist sling, nickering frantically for reassurance.

The prince clouted Lord Artos affectionately on the shoulder. "I believe you now, Artos—for I had my doubts before, I'll be frank. But these are splendid animals." Then he leaned closer to the *Comes*. "How long do you think it will be before we all can be mounted on such warhorses as these?"

I was struck by the look that suffused the features of the *Comes Britannorum*, that look of far seeing: not of trance or dream, but of a reality waiting just ahead of him. "Five, six, seven years, and there won't be a warrior without a black horse of this quality to carry him to battle against the Saxons. A stallion such as Cornix here can cover thirty, forty, maybe fifty mares without loss of fertility. And these are eager to do their duty. Each of the mares is also in foal, so any colts may also stand if they're up to the standard I mean to have."

"Aye, the Saxons will have to beware!" And the prince's expression turned grim. He pulled Artos to one side for private conversation. Out of the corner of my eye—for I was busy feeding the mare hanks of grass pulled from the roadside—I could see all the elation of success bleed from the *Comes*'s face. I was saddened to see the change.

Suddenly my shoulder was seized in a fierce and painful grip. Startled, I tried first to twist free, and then to see who had made me captive.

"I have you, Galwyn Varianus!" Dolcenus bellowed, and there was no escaping the grip of the big, burly port officer. "Scurrilous wretch! Runaway apprentice! You'll come with me, vile ingrate, and stay in the lockup until your uncle returns."

It was too late for me to rue my stupidity. I should have known that Dolcenus would arrive to see what manner of strange cargo was being hoisted ashore in his precinct. I would have been safe aboard the ship; now my brave adventure was at an end. I could almost feel the manacles of a galley slave tightening about my wrists.

It was in fact Bericus's huge hand that prevented Dolcenus from hauling me summarily away. That and the now-frightened mare whose lead rope I still held. She reared and Dolcenus released me, shouting at the top of his lungs for me to be recaptured immediately, and yelling for help against this resistance to his authority.

"What goes?" I heard Lord Artos cry.

"If you harm one of those mares, Dolcenus . . ." Prince Cador roared.

And the mare reared again.

Fortunately, Bericus was beside me and together we calmed her, despite the cries and imprecations that colored the air. Her alarm had infected the stallion and the nickering pony. I had to dance out of the way of the foal, who was trying to get under his dam's belly for safety.

It took the combined authority of both prince and *Comes* Artos to restore order. Then they heard Dolcenus's charge against me while I stood, head down, too humiliated to look beyond the belts of the men encircling me.

"It was my understanding," Lord Artos said when Dolcenus paused in his litany of my sins to draw breath, "that Captain Gralior dispatched the boy to be of assistance in our journey. In truth, Galwyn had already been of great help. Knowing that Gralior was due to sail, I had asked if I might have the loan of the boy while Gralior was at sea. The boy has knowledge of so many barbarous languages. How was it, Galwyn, that you joined us?"

When I could not answer, *Comes* Artos put his hand under my chin and forced me to look at him. Unmanly tears trickled down my cheeks and I could not speak for fear of blubbering.

"He came on a pony, with a travel cloak and leggings," Bericus said stoutly. I felt his encouraging hand on my shoulder blade, one hard thumb poking me to speak.

"He's a thief as well?" cried Dolcenus. "Branded he must be!"

"Nonsense," Prince Cador said. "I knew the boy's father. Too honorable, too Roman a family to breed thieves. He resisted the temptation to flee to Armorica. Speak up, lad."

"Aye, speak, lad," and Lord Artos's voice was as

kind as his eyes, when at last I dared glance up at them.

"I bought Spadix with the small gold ring Tegidus thanked me with."

"You see, Dolcenus, this boy's no thief!" said Bericus.

"And the cloak and leggings with the coins you were kind enough to send me, Lord Artos! Please, I want to serve *you, Comes Britannorum*." And I dropped to my knees in the dust, as much because my legs would no longer hold me up as to plead my cause with proper humility. "It is the horses of the land that I know, not the sea!"

"Is the boy a free man?" Lord Artos asked Dolcenus.

The man sputtered and stammered.

"Yes, my lord, I am free. I was only apprenticed to my uncle, not enslaved." I glared at Dolcenus to make him speak the truth.

"That is correct," Prince Cador said when Dolcenus still would not speak for frustration. "I remember the case of Decitus Varianus now. He acted honorably in his circumstances."

"The boy's too good with his tongue to be lost to a barge captain, Lord Artos," said Bericus. "And he's got a fine way with seasick horses!"

"Horses!" cried Lord Artos, grabbing me up from the ground. "We can just make the evening tide if we hurry. Bericus, I'll leave you in charge."

"He is my guest," Prince Cador said quickly, and Artos raised his hand, grinning, in appreciation of the offer. "There's a field not far"—and he pointed up the straight track that led from the harbor—"where the horses can be tended until you've brought the rest across the sea. My hostlers can help him with this lot."

"I'll count them every morning, Artos," Bericus said with a broad grin, "to be sure they're all present and accounted for."

Prince Cador laughed. "Oh, I can wait, good Bericus, until I'm offered one."

"You'll join me, then, to drive the Saxons from our lands?" Artos said, with a leap of relief in his voice.

"You couldn't keep me away, Artos," Cador replied. "Now, we'll just get these poor sea-wrecked creatures to a decent pasture and then we'll await your return."

Artos then placed his hand again on Cador's shoulder. "Good prince, make what provision is needed to salve the uncle's wounded pride, and give this port officer something for his attention to duty. Young Galwyn, you come with me!" He transferred his big hand to my shoulder and hauled me along beside him back to the captain. "Can we make the evening tide? You've taken aboard supplies?"

"Even as you ordered, *Comes*," the captain said staunchly, pointing to crewmen loading while others were hammering the deck boards back into place.

WE MADE A SWIFT PASSAGE back to Burtigala with both ships, but the next return voyage was rougher and took its toll on man and beast. One foal broke a foreleg and had to be destroyed. Lord Artos himself severed its jugular vein, not wanting anyone else to have such a sad duty. Then the foal was heaved overboard. Its mare was so miserable, desperately trying to keep her balance, that she was not aware of the loss of her foal. A sailor swabbed the blood off the deck within minutes.

I was far too busy looking after the mares and my lord Artos to have time to be seasick. When we reached the port on the Exe River again, there were messages awaiting Lord Artos such that he could not accompany us on the third trip.

"Galwyn," he said when we had the beasts safely on the shore, "had I more men like you, I'd be sure of driving the Saxons forever from our lands."

"I thought, Lord Artos, it was the horses you needed to do that," I said, so relieved that I hazarded an impudence.

"The horses need men to ride them, Galwyn: men such as you!" And he clamped his great hand on my shoulder, his eyes gleaming with his fervor.

"My loyalty, my heart, my soul are yours, *Comes* Artos," I replied, dropping to my knee and bringing the hem of his garment to my forehead in an act of fealty, "to do with as you will."

He raised me to my feet, his eyes fastened on mine. "With men such as you, Galwyn Varianus, on horses such as these, we will be invincible!"

I trembled, as much with relief that he accepted my oath as from weariness. And he saw that, too.

"Enough of talk. You men are all exhausted." To be called a man by the *Comes*? I straightened my weary self. He went on. "Come, I've rooms for you, Bwlch, and the others for the night. And here are Bericus and some of Cador's men to help with the horses. They will need to be rested, but Cador has put a field at our disposal until we have them all here. Then what a cavalcade they will make on the road to Deva! I can hardly wait to see old Rhodri's eyes when they light on these fine steeds."

Part Two

THE ROAD
TO DEVA

THE THIRD AND FINAL VOYAGE was the best and the worst.

The best because Lord Artos put me in charge of the horses on one ship—Bwlch was on the other. I was both proud of the honor and fearful of failure.

The worst because we caught the brunt of a fierce autumnal gale for the first two days. Somehow we, and the horses, survived, though all of us were bruised and exhausted. The horses were barely able to drink water when it was offered them. With tattered sails, our two ships limped up the mist-covered Exe to the wharf.

These crossings to collect the precious stallions and mares had taken us well into the tenth month, and into the misty and often chill weather of the season. So we weren't surprised by the fog.

Some keen-eyed watcher must have spotted us despite the weather and sent word, because we had barely secured the ships to the bollards when Bericus came charging off of the mist-shrouded dock on my Spadix. His long legs stuck straight out in front of the pony so they would not trail on the ground. Spadix snorted and came to a stop just as the last deck plank was removed.

"Thought you might like to see your old friend, Galwyn," Bericus called cheerfully, planting his legs on the ground and all but walking straight off the pony. "Besides"—and his grin was full of mischief—"old Canyd won't let any of the Libyans be ridden yet."

"Who's Canyd?" I asked.

Bericus grinned. "He knows all the ails and aches a horse can have and how to cure them."

This latest shipment of Libyan horses, heads hanging down with exhaustion, were not as troublesome coming out of the ship as they had been going in. Of course, Bwlch, Bericus, and I were by now experienced in such transfers, so this one was accomplished speedily. And the men Prince Cador had promised arrived. Each hostler took charge of a weary animal, some of whom were barely able to put one shaky foot in front of the other now they were back on solid ground.

Reins hitched to a nearby bollard, Spadix gave little encouraging nickers. Whatever he said to the poor creatures, they seemed to prick their ears a bit and whuffle softly, as if reassured by both his presence and his comments.

Finally, all the horses were safely ashore and Bericus checked each of them.

"Their legs have stocked up with fluid," he said, not in the least perturbed. "But some rest and liniments of old Canyd Bawn's making will soon set them right." He clasped my shoulder. "You did well, lad. Very well indeed."

His words were salve to the effects of sleepless nights and long watches.

"And I did not?" Bwlch asked in mock outrage.

"I expect it of you, Bwlch," Bericus said, with a grin to take the sting out of his words. "Now let's get these poor creatures to the pasture before they fall down on the hard wharf stones."

I moved to take up the lead rope of one of the mares, but Bericus's big hand on my arm stopped me. He turned me and gave me a little push toward Spadix. "You ride, lad. You're as liable to fall as one of the horses. You'll get your land legs back soon, never fear."

I must admit that I was relieved to be able to ride. The road, ascending steeply from the harbor and disappearing into the swirling mist, looked more than my wobbly legs could handle. I scrambled astride Spadix with considerable relief and took the lead rope of one of the tottery mares.

By the time we reached the top of the steep hill, where we crossed the eastbound military road, the mist had dispersed and the day was bright and clear. The harbor seemed completely resident in another land.

Sighting his field companions, Spadix whickered loudly, announcing the new arrivals. They answered by charging up to the fence to see who was approaching. Horses are curious herd animals and like to do things together. Once again, I was taken with a surge of pride to be part of *Comes* Artos's great dream.

No dream creatures these, pawing at the ground and pressing their broad chests against the restraining rails. These were solid reality. The foals born to them next spring would be just as fine.

The newcomers, who had wobbled courageously up the hill, now cocked their ears forward, appreciating the audience and glad to be back in the herd that they had formed since leaving Septimania. They even stepped out more surely across the road, sensing the end of their long and momentous journey.

From the small shelter built inside the pasture, several men emerged to greet and inspect the new arrivals. I noticed one man in particular, his one shoulder badly crooked, perhaps from an old injury. His angular face wore a slight smile and his eyes a measuring gaze as he looked from one weary horse to another. Or, to be precise, he looked at their legs. Shaking his head, he returned to the shelter and came out again with a bucket.

"They be worse than t'others," he said gloomily to Bericus, who was bringing in his charge, the fourth of the stallions, Victor.

"They are, but I've every faith in your ability to set them right, Canyd."

"Whyn't you bring 'em to me in good shape, and then we'd be on our way out of here?" grumbled Canyd.

I watched as he ran a gentle, knowing hand down the sweaty stallion's shoulder. Then he hunkered to examine the swollen legs. He clicked his tongue, shaking his head as he rose, his eyes on Victor's deep chest and wide barrel. Lightly he ran his hands everywhere, as if making sure the stallion would recognize him ever after from his touch and his soft "Sa-sa-sa."

Victor brought his head up, twisting it around to follow Canyd's progress. When the old man came forward again, his hand held flat under the stallion's nose, he placed both hands on the horse's muzzle and blew into his nostrils, a trick I had seen my father's head groom do with new animals. Victor had the scent of the man now.

Canyd went from one horse to the next, checking them over carefully, his tongue continually clicking or making soothing *sa-sa* noises. I was fascinated by his manner and method; so were the horses, who seemed to recognize him instantly as someone who would do them no hurt.

"All right," he said finally, coming back to his bucket, which I saw held cloths soaking in a liquid. It had an astringent smell to it. "Gather 'round, ye louts. Y'ought by now to know how to tend these poor legs. I want every one of 'em stooped, properly, now. And I'll do this fine lad."

He looked up at brown Victor, smiling to himself in approval.

"What're you standin' about for, lad? Get busy," he said, nodding at me and then at the nearest mare. "Nestor, Yayin, Donan, have at it, an' let's make these poor storm-tossed beasties comfortable."

So I fell to with the others, my own weariness sloughed off with the need to tend my charges.

While I bathed the swollen legs of Dorcas, the mare I had led, Spadix wandered off, grazing here and there until he found a patch of ground that met with his approval. He dropped to his knees with a huge groan, threw his head down, and began to roll backward and forward, rubbing his backbone against the ground to ease his muscles.

I heard Canyd's soft chuckle. "Worth a gold ring for every full turn he makes. Worth a lot, that 'un."

Spadix got to his feet again and shook himself from nose to tail. His exercise completed, he fell to grazing as if that had been his prime object in the first place.

Myself, I wondered if a good roll on the hard ground would help the unsettled feeling I still had: that a ship's deck was rocking beneath my feet. Once or twice I had to grab at the mare to steady myself. At least she had four legs to prop herself on: "One in each corner," as Solvin, my father's old hostler, used to say—generally about a horse that he felt lacked any other redeeming quality. Dorcas was so enjoying having her legs bathed that she didn't even notice my grasping.

"Now, lad, that'll do for her," Canyd said, startling me because I had been concentrating on my task and also preventing myself from rolling onto the ground. "There's a fine cold stream at the end of the pasture, an' later you can stand her in that. The steeping will take down the filling in short order."

I saw that the others had finished and were assembled by the brazier in front of the shelter. Bericus joined us there.

"I've lodgings for you and Bwlch in the village," he said, clapping me on the shoulder again in a most friendly fashion. "And a hot meal, which you certainly deserve. Soon enough you'll take your turn as sentry here, but now get your pony. I doubt you'd make the trip on your own legs. Bwlch's swaying like he's in a high wind, and you're not much better."

I flushed, deploring my weakness, but his hand tightened briefly on my shoulder and I could see the concern in his eyes.

That was when I noticed the narrowed gaze of a slightly built lad not much taller or older than myself. He was staring across the brazier fire. A Cornovian: His glance was surly, his narrow head cocked to one side as he appraised me, and his thin mouth turned down in a supercilious sneer. I was to learn shortly that his name was Iswy. My first impression of him was of a sly and devious fellow, envious of any attentions that he did not get to share. I never had occasion to change my opinion when our tasks put us in closer association. Then Bericus gestured for me to follow him, Bwlch only too grateful to come with us.

Perhaps it was Iswy's hostile attitude, or maybe the return into the concealing fog that had not yet been burned off by the morning sun, but I felt apprehensive as we walked down the shrouded way. The fog closed in behind us and I shivered.

As we neared the wharf again, the mist on the water was thinning, but my apprehension increased—as if Iswy's glance still followed me. Several times I looked around furtively at the people passing us on their daily tasks: a baker with his tray of bread, some fishermen with heavy creels, a tanner trotting along, the hides of his burden strapped to his back.

"What do you expect to see over your shoulder, Galwyn?" Bericus asked good-humoredly. "That uncle of yours?" When he saw my startled reaction he added immediately, "Ah, lad, I'm to see that he doesn't trouble you for any reason. You're one of us now, you know."

"I'm at your side as well," Bwlch said so staunchly that I relaxed.

"Fog makes me nervous, too," Bericus added, and then guided us into the next thatched building.

From the smell of old beer and wine, I knew the ground floor acted as *taberna* though it was empty at this time of the day, save for a slave sweeping the floor. Bericus led us to the stairs on one long end, and we could hear a confusion of voices and much clanging of pots coming from the kitchen annex. The loft divided into rough sleeping quarters, and it was into one of the two front ones that Bericus led us. Eight pallets of straw laid on rough bedsteads limited our walking space, but Bericus made an expansive gesture.

"Take your pick and I shall keep anyone from disturbing you until you've slept yourselves out." With that he disappeared.

Bwlch dropped to the nearest bed, stuffing the bag of his belongings under it before he lay flat on the mattress. He gave a huge sigh and, I think, was asleep in the next instant. I was equally glad to lay myself down, although I could not compose myself quite as readily for sleep as Bwlch had. The bed, too, rocked under me, and probably rocked me to sleep as well—for I heard nothing until Bericus roused us to eat our evening meal.

"But I should have stooped the mare's legs!" I cried, sitting bolt upright on the straw.

Bericus and Bwlch both laughed, and I saw two others beyond them smiling at my confusion.

"All done, and to Canyd's close satisfaction," Bericus said. "Tomorrow is soon enough for you to take up your duties. We've a feast tonight—the coin I gave the landlord should ensure one—to celebrate the safe arrival—"

"Safe? When we lost the foal . . ." I began, conscience-stricken.

"Galwyn"—and Bericus put his hand on my shoulder to stem my denial—"he has no idea, has he, Bwlch"—and he grinned at the other Companion—"how well he did to bring so many safely ashore? No, lad, to lose only one is well indeed. Even Prince Cador was amazed at our good fortune. And envious of our fine herd!"

"As well he should be," Bwlch said, and then we all bustled down to the inn, where rough trestle tables had been set up with a fine meal upon them, roast suckling pig and three capons, as well as mounds of vegetables and loaves of bread.

"Eat hearty, Galwyn," Bericus urged. "Travel food is not such as this, and we've a long journey to Deva."

I followed his advice and gorged myself until I thought I would burst. I did not, however, eat until my stomach overflowed, as did Decius Gallicanus and the sour-faced Cornovian Egdyl the White; I knew this was the custom at feasts, a remnant of Roman habits.

The two beakers of well-watered wine that Bericus fixed for me probably accounted for the reason I was able to sleep not three hours after rising from a daylong rest. Cheerfully he advised me to sleep as deeply as I could, for I'd be camping out from tomorrow on.

CAMPING OUT WOULD HAVE BEEN no problem to me, had it not been for the attitude of Iswy, Decius, and Egdyl. Very quickly they made it obvious to me that I was merely a horse boy now, and the lowest of that lowly rank.

"Here, you boy," Iswy said as if he were my superior. "Shovel up these droppings."

"He can help me carry water to the footsore," Decius spoke up, probably thinking that as the older man, he had a better right to dispose of my time.

I shrugged. I was quite willing to do either task, and I looked for guidance from Canyd.

"Give him one job or t'other," Canyd said. "Tho' it's your horse who made the pile, Iswy," he added, and dismissed me to assist Decius.

Their attitude became even harsher on those days when Bericus took me to help him with errands, as if I weren't working just as hard with the Companion as I would have under Canyd's orders. At that, I would have much rather stayed on in the camp to watch Canyd's way with horses—for he was uncanny. Every single horse, Cornix included, would come when he called. He would stand by his bucket of lotion and they would approach, waiting patiently while he examined them daily, from poll to tail. And all that after each groom had already checked his charge at morning feed.

The droppings of the newest ones were very loose after they began to graze. Of course, at this time of year grass had not the nutritive value of, say, the first vernal growth, but it was juicier than the dry hay that we supplied them at night. Canyd inspected each pile in the field, checking for worms, the remedy for which was a clove of garlic mashed into their crushed oats.

"It's the new grass, the new water, as upsets their

innards," Canyd told me. "So far they've all come around, even the mares in foal. I'd some worry for them, making such a wild trip an' all. But they be sturdy. Their feet are good, too."

"Feet?" I exclaimed, since the conformation of the animals was most notable in their deep chests and barrels, the bones of their legs.

"No foot, no horse," Canyd said.

I confess that I stared for a moment at the man, suddenly recalling Lord Artos using the same words. So here was the man who wanted to put an iron rim on horses' feet. I knew, of course, that it was necessary to be sure no stones or thorns were stuck in the frog of the foot, and I'd carved myself a little prod for just that purpose. But a sandal of iron for a horse?

"'Tis not just stones y'kin worry about wi' fine horses." He beckoned me to the nearest mare and pointed at her long hoof. "See?"

I tried to see what he was pointing out to me but did not until he tapped on and traced with a gnarled fingertip a slight ridge on her horny hoof. "That's a growth ring. She had a bad year then but it's growing out. We'll see that none other grows in."

I stored that bit of knowledge away, as I was storing practically every word Canyd said. If I was to be of use to *Comes* Artos, I had to learn all I could about the care of his Libyan horses.

WHILE THE LATEST ARRIVALS were getting their land legs and accustoming their stomachs to the good British grass, there was much to do in preparation for the journey.

Bericus patronized merchants in both the village and the larger town near the old Roman fort, established at the first ford of the River Exe, well beyond its navigable reaches. Bericus had the use of one of Prince Cador's horses, and I rode Spadix on the outward journeys, though the pony was often laden with supplies on the way back, with me walking at his head.

Bericus knew a great deal more about provisioning a long land journey than I did, though I had helped my uncle bargain for ship's food in many Gallic ports. Bericus was also a soldier, so it was legion fare for which he haggled with his chain of gold rings. We would be eating wheat spelt, which was cheap and in good quantity at this time of the autumn.

I noticed that Bericus was most particular about the oats he bought for the horses, running his hands through the sacks to check the dustiness of the grain. Too much dust, and a horse could develop a bad cough. He demanded the best of the tanners' wares, too, for we had to be sure the halters were sturdy enough to control our charges. Each of us would ride one and lead one, with pack ponies for our provisions.

Then, knowing that I stood up in all my possessions, Bericus found an oiled cape and a thick woolen tunic for me. Gone were the days when I worried about the fall of my tunic or what color to dye my sandal straps. The leggings and sandals that I had bought for myself in Burtigala showed few signs of wear yet, so I thought myself well provided for. I did use a quarter of the second ring Tegidus had given me to pay a carter who was traveling to where my mother and my two sisters were living, near the fort at Ide, to carry a letter to reassure them. I had no illusions about my uncle's kindness. Out of spite, he was as likely to tell them that I had drowned at sea as he was to admit that I had bettered myself in the entourage of Lord Artos.

While these forays gave me a respite from Iswy's snide remarks and Decius's notion that I should help him with his share of the chores, I had also to deal on my return with the envy such excursions caused. Egdyl then began to order me about, too.

"The fire needs tending, boy," Egdyl said when I had just settled myself at the hearth for an evening meal the others were already eating. "Lively, now."

The man had exactly my uncle's manner and I could feel myself resisting.

"You can reach a log from where you sit, Egdyl," Canyd said, and motioned for me to stay seated. He handed me my bowl of soup and a bannock of *blaanda* bread.

Ignoring me completely, Egdyl, Decius, and Iswy talked about friends at Prince Cador's farms, frequently lapsing into Celtic. I may have been taught to speak a purer Latin than they, but I could follow the Celtic as easily, though I acted as if I could not. Once or twice, Iswy would mockingly slip in a phrase I customarily used. He had also taken to mimicking me, echoing the words I'd used in questions to Canyd.

My father had always taught me to bide my time instead of making abrupt judgments of either men or horses. The months with my uncle had taught me other lessons: how to survive as the lowliest of the crew, and how to recognize bullies. The long happy weeks with Lord Artos had sufficiently restored my self-esteem so that I would not, could not, return to the wretched, bullied existence I had endured on the *Corellia* and be the butt of jokes and the recipient of spite. I had no idea how I might reverse Iswy's opinion of me—if, indeed, I could—but it was obvious that I would suffer his unfriendly attentions the entire way to Deva. That did not suit me. But I had to be careful how I called him to task, or I would suffer the loss of Bericus's kind interest.

The others who made up the twenty-man escort of the black Libyan horses were the sort who would get on with any job of work that was set them: Five were soldiers of *Comes* Artos's legion and chosen for their skill in horsemanship. Six had been lent by Prince Cador for the same reason. Canyd Bawn was the *Comes*'s man and had come down from Deva especially to help the fine new steeds travel. He had brought with him three men. They were not unfriendly but they sat somewhat apart from the other two groups, who were more apt to mingle than the Devans. I was neither fish nor fowl: not high enough in rank to intrude on the Companions, nor naturally included with any of the others.

However, I came to the conclusion that it was Canyd whose goodwill I needed most. Gaining his respect would mean strict attention to his orders about the care of the horses. He was not the sort who bantered with others around the campfire, where he, like I did for another reason, listened intently without comment.

By the end of the first week, Bericus was eager to

start the journey, but he had to wait until Canyd would allow the horses to proceed.

"They're fine animals, sir," Canyd said, cocking his head. "But that mare, now, she's a touch colicky with the strange grass scratching her belly. I wouldn't want to start the journey with her liable to come down. Wouldn't do for her to tie up her guts . . ."

"But when they're colicky, you walk them. Why not walk them out on the journey?" Bericus asked.

"It's not only the lass I worry about, sir, but yon stallion—Victor, you call him. He hasn't settled to his food and nothing pleases him. No condition back on his bones yet, and that's not good for a long journey either, not when we'll be changing grass and water holes every night. It's a long way to Deva from here."

"We can take hay from here and feed him that on the road," Bericus suggested.

Canyd raised one gnarled finger in warning. "As well to wait a day or two more and see him settled than go through all that rigamarole."

"It'll be a long-enough journey, and the weather none too clement this time of the year . . ."

"True, true," Canyd said, nodding affably. "A day or two more is all."

Bericus sighed but was obviously bound by Canyd's advice. Then he cast me a significant look, nodding toward Spadix, and when it occurred to me that this was Sunday, I understood. We mounted, and some distance farther on the road were joined by Bwlch, also on his way to the little church in Isca. There, I am sure, all our prayers were to have a safe journey—soon!

If, on my return, I caught snide looks and remarks, I

71

had retained sufficient joy from the mass to ignore them. I would have thought that some of Cador's men were Christian, for there were many monasteries in Cordovici, though I remembered some talk around the campfires about how many had divorced themselves from Roman ways when the legions had not come to our assistance.

WE PREPARED TO DEPART two days later, at dawn, gathering for the last time around the fire, our gear all tied and ready. Bericus unfolded a parchment map, tilted it toward the light, and glanced at me, for he knew that I had been taught to read. By such an action, sadly, he left me open to more jibes by those who could not.

"There are forts and villas along this road where we will be welcome," he said, one finger pointing the direction we would take. "We will not always have to sleep out, but always"—and he paused, looking around at everyone—"always the safety of the horses is the first priority. We have over three hundred *mille passus* to go, and Lord Artos has allowed three weeks to accomplish the journey, barring accidents." Again he gave a keen glance of his pale eyes around the circle. "We will *have* no accidents." The response was hearty from most of his listeners, though I caught Iswy's sly look and the skeptical one that Gallicanus gave Egdyl. The three men from Deva—Nestor, Yayin, and Donan—looked far more optimistic, but they knew the road, having just traveled it to Isca.

The journey to Deva would certainly be less dangerous than our way from Burtigala to Septimania down the wide Garuma Valley, for we would be among our own people, people who had good reason to wish Lord Artos's project to succeed. That, I was sure, did not quite keep Bericus from worrying about those who would like to acquire such fine animals for their own.

"Now, I will assign you your mount and your lead for the first day. We may shuffle these assignments about"—and here he grinned—"as we discover each other's capabilities. The mares with foals afoot are to be led, and so is that black demon of a stallion Lord Artos is so fond of." Bericus's grin broadened. He shot an amused glance at those who had been favored by the stallion's fractious manners. Only Canyd had been able to do much with him. Now Bericus turned to me. "Galwyn, you'll lead Cornix from your pony, for I've seen him trot as placid as a mare in Spadix's company."

Once again, and without meaning to, Bericus had made me the butt of envy—though, at that moment, I could feel my chest swell with pride to be given such a position of trust. I glanced at Iswy, whose black look made me shudder. There were murmurs of surprise. Difficult as the stallion was, it was still considered an honor to attend the beast.

"Galwyn led him often enough on our journey from Septimania when the Comes did not ride him," Bericus went on by way of explanation.

"And what if the beast smells a mare in season on the road?" Decius Gallicanus asked. "Is the boy strong enough to hold him?"

Bericus grinned back. "No man is strong enough to hold that fellow when he wants to do otherwise. Even Comes Artos had his hands full."

"I've a bit he will respect," said Canyd Bawn, in his reedy voice. "Not that any man would object to having his mare served by such like," he added with an amused snort. He winked at me. "Lad, I'll show you how a yank or two will change the mind of that *diabolus* about pulling away from you."

I was more than grateful for such consideration, and heaved a sigh. Leading the black stallion would be hazardous, but with Spadix's calming influence, I was reasonably confident I could manage him.

I only half listened to the other assignments.

"We pull out at dawn," Bericus said in conclusion, and dismissed us to our duties.

AT DAWN, A CHILLY AUTUMNAL rain began, which augered ill for the journey and made me doubly grateful for the oiled cloth cloak. I could also have used one of the broad hats that Prince Cador's men had, to prevent the rain from trickling down the collar and my neck. The rain had a dampening effect on Cornix, who plodded along beside Spadix as meek as a sheep. I had no need to use the heavy metal bit that Canyd had managed to set between his jaws. It was a wicked-looking thing to my eyes, with a jaw-breaking gag and a port that would bear up against the roof of his mouth—if I jerked hard enough on the lead rope—to give him something painful to think about. I got so I hated to force that atrocity into his mouth.

We proceeded at a pace that even Victor could manage. Our passage churned the eastern road out of Isca into a thick mud that forced us to go at a slow walk. We'd not cover many *stadia* in such treacherous

74

going at that pace. I was thoroughly miserable, and my thighs were rubbed raw by the wet pad on Spadix's back.

"Perhaps the going will get better," Nestor remarked when we paused for Bericus to pry clay and stones out of the off-front foot of the stallion he was riding. "'Specially when we reach the old paved road." He paused. "I doubt we'll get there tomorrow. It's some eighteen *mille passus* beyond Isca. After that, it's north toward Lindinis, and we'll have good road all the way from Lindinis to Aqua Sulis."

I'd heard of Aqua Sulis, a big fortified town, from the traders who stopped at my father's villa. It had been a Legion fortress and was supposed still to have hot baths, which the Romans had deemed essential to a proper lifestyle. There had been many fine villas nearby. I wondered if we'd be lucky enough to pass a night at one. And if, considering how I would be taunted by Iswy, I'd have the courage to *take* a hot bath, were one offered.

We plodded onward until the winter's early dusk caught us, far from the first stopping point on Bericus's map. So we camped in a dense copse of trees, near a small stream. There each of us had to wash the legs of our mounts and, under the scrutiny of Canyd, check for tendons strained by the muddy going and be certain the hooves were clear of any pebbles that might cause lameness. One or two of the mares seemed to have a little heat in their legs, so Canyd brought out his arnica lotion, which could reduce swelling and heat.

One of the three men from Deva—Nestor, a thin little man with bowed legs—was also the cook. He carried enough dry wood in one of his many bundles to heat the thin vinegary wine that legionnaires drank, but we ate our pease porridge cold. I found that dish quite tasty, though the others grumbled. Then we rolled up in our blankets and got such sleep as the conditions allowed. I think I did better than most, having got accustomed to sleeping on the stormy decks of cold ships. I had also reacquired land legs and the ground under me no longer had even the slightest rocking motion.

More pease porridge in the morning, but there'd be rabbit for dinner. Nestor had laid snares the night before, having seen signs of rabbit, and his traps had caught four. Not to be outdone, Iswy brought down five plump pigeons with his sling during the morning. He was incredibly accurate, and he took every opportunity to show off his prowess, even shooting down small birds that had no value for the pot at all.

Though we had other rainy days, we never ate cold food in the evening again. The rivalry between the different groups over supplying the kettle became a matter of honor. As the youngest member, I didn't get the choicer bits, but I wouldn't give anyone the satisfaction of hearing me complain. Occasionally, I was also able to contribute. One evening, I gathered apples from a deserted orchard we passed. And another day, I found cress by a fast-moving stream and nuts windlost from walnut trees.

Whenever we passed a stretch of water that was banked by willows, Canyd insisted that we pause long enough to strip bark from the saplings.

"'Tis hard enough to come by when it's needed," he

said. "The trees be soon asleep, so this is the last chance this year." Carefully he rolled the bark into a wallet he kept for that purpose. "Grand for fevers, it is. Sovereign remedy for aches and pains."

I should comment here that, although we met few travelers on the road, those we did meet were amazed by the size of our horses. And envious. But the sight of Prince Cador's armed men, as well as Bericus's casual mention that *Comes* Artos owned the horses, dissuaded anyone from trying to part us from our mounts.

In fact, several small parties of traders asked to join our band for safety's sake. Raiders from Ireland were not uncommon in this area, and one elderly trader remarked bleakly that he had moved westward since the Saxons had raided too often and too close to Eburacum for his peace of mind, much less any profit. Morning and evening, he also continually increased the number of gold rings he offered Bericus to purchase one of the Libyans. He ended up offering a staggering price for one of the foals if none of the mares would be sold him—though he also complained he would have to wait three long years for his purchase to be worth what he was giving.

We had to pass three days at Corinium when the youngest of the stallions, the one we called Paphin, was kicked by a mare he tried to mount. Once again, it was Canyd's potions that set him right. I was fascinated by Canyd's fund of knowledge. Old Solvin would have listened as closely as I.

Paying attention to the old man's "sermons"— which is how Iswy sneeringly referred to Canyd's

descriptions of the treatments—did nothing to ingra-
tiate me with the others.

ISWY WAS AN EXCELLENT RIDER, as tight to the
back of his mare as a limpet to a ship's hull. He
had good hands as well, and certainly a feel for a horse,
but riding was his obsession: preferably having a
chance to back every horse in our cavalcade. He especially wanted a chance to ride Cornix, because no one
else had.

I didn't quite realize how desperately he wanted that
chance until I overheard him pleading with Bericus. I
was returning from a call of nature when his voice,
raised in supplication, drifted toward me.

"The horse needs to be ridden, Lord Bericus," Iswy
was saying in a wheedling tone. I ducked aside from
the path so as not to be seen listening. "Lord Artos
would want him to be ridden."

"Lord Artos will do whatever riding that horse
needs, Iswy."

"But I can stay on anything." The nasal whine of
Iswy's scratchy voice must have annoyed Bericus as
much as it did me.

"That may be true enough, Iswy, but I have specific
instructions from Lord Artos, and Galwyn will continue to lead him."

"I could do that as well, Lord Bericus."

"Your offer is appreciated, Iswy." Bericus was obviously moving away from him, because his voice
became less distinct.

There was a silence while I stood motionless, lest
Iswy know that I had overheard his humiliation. Then

he began a flow of soft cursing such as I had never heard before—vicious, promising vengeance from pagan gods on the high and mighty Lord Bericus for denying Iswy his simple request.

I crept back into the camp shaken with apprehension by the malice in his words. I had no doubts at all that he would try to do something irrational and perhaps dangerous, but I did not know what to do about warning Bericus.

I doubled my vigilance, sleeping that night near Cornix's end of the picket line.

I observed nothing unusual. The next morning, however, Spadix's near foreleg was swollen to the knee and he would not even put his hoof tip to the ground. I couldn't imagine what he could have done, for he had been sound the night before. He was such a sturdy pony that he 'was the one least likely to have leg trouble. As I raced for Canyd, seated by the fire with his porridge, I caught just a glimpse of Iswy's face—and the malicious smile on it.

I faltered in my headlong dash for Canyd, suddenly realizing that even that clever man would be unable to cure my pony before we had to be on the road again that morning. Exactly what Iswy wanted. I would not be able to lead Cornix from a seat on Spadix, so the animal would have to be ridden. And Iswy was acknowledged to be the best rider of us all.

"What is it, lad?" Canyd cried, looking up from his porridge bowl.

"Spadix." And I tugged at Canyd's arm. Maybe he had something heroic to cure my pony. "It's his leg. Swole up like a wasps' nest."

"It is?" Canyd rose in one swift movement, putting his bowl aside as he did so, surprise and confusion on his face.

"Oh, come quickly. He won't even put his toe to the ground." I pulled on Canyd's thin wiry arm.

"Easy, lad, easy," Canyd said, patting my hands to ease their grip on his arm. "I'm comin', I'm comin'."

Spadix was beyond Cornix on the picket, and his swollen leg was visible as we approached.

"*Sa-sa*, lad," Canyd said, touching Spadix's rump with a gentle hand as he moved in beside him and crouched by the filled leg. "*Sa-sa*, now what have ye don' to yursel'?"

"He didn't do anything, Canyd. It was done *to* him!"

Canyd paused in his examination and squinted up at me. "It was, was it? This pony's that tired he swole his leg up so as not to lead out Cornix today?" And Canyd winked at me.

Astonished, I was speechless as I watched the wise hands gently press against the leg. Spadix nickered low in pain and tossed his head nervously. I went to his head and began stroking his muzzle, murmuring my own "*Sa-sa*"s to reassure him. I was proud of being part of those tending Lord Artos's marvelous horses; but Spadix was mine, and his injury, as spiteful as it was, distressed me more than I thought possible. Before my father's heart had failed him, I had had the best ponies money could buy, but I had never felt the kinship with them that I felt for this shaggy plebeian fellow.

Canyd kept up his "*Sa-sa*" while he felt more deeply in the leg, felt the hoof itself; and then, with his head practically on the ground because the swelling in the fetlock prevented the pony from tipping his hoof, he looked at the underside of it.

"Hmmmm"—and Canyd pressed both thumbs hard on the frog. Spadix did not react to the pressure. "Not hot. Not sore. That's good."

Spadix nodded his head vigorously, as if agreeing. Canyd continued his careful examination: the outside of the hoof again, up to the coronary band; and there, his knowing fingers stopped.

"We didna' go through thorny bushes, did we, lad?" he asked, of the pony more than of me.

I shook my head vigorously. "We were on roadway all day and I checked his legs last night as I always do. His and Cornix's. He was sound last night, Master Canyd, he was sound." I tried not to let my voice break but it did, and then a gentle finger prodded me.

"Did I say 'twas your fault, lad? Nay. But . . ." And he set his thumb and forefingers carefully to pulling a triangular thorn from the flesh beside the sesamoid bone. With narrowed eyes, he peered at it a long moment and then pushed it at me.

"How could—I mean, it just doesn't—!" I exclaimed, examining the wicked triangle.

"Indeed, lad, an' how a clever-footed pony like this 'un could possibly get such a thorn in his leg is beyond Canyd's understanding. We won't talk about that now. *Sa?*" He cocked his head at me in a cautionary pose. Winked again. "Now get me hot water, my bag, an' some bran from the sack. We must poultice it to draw the infection." His voice followed me as I ran to do his bidding.

Had I encountered Iswy on my way I'm not sure

what I would have done to the fiend. And he was supposed to be such a great horseman! No *real* horseman would deliberately injure a horse. Or a pony.

We had the poultice wrapped around the swollen foreleg when Bericus came over to inquire what was wrong. I started to rise, to blurt out my suspicions, when Canyd pinched my leg so hard I had to grab Spadix's good leg to keep from tipping over.

"Bad?" Bericus asked Canyd, who nodded solemnly. "What?"

"Thorn." And Canyd gave a diffident shrug.

"Wouldn't you know!" Bericus sighed, glancing at me—but not in an accusing sort of way: more as if this delay were one more trial to be overcome. Then he strode back to the fire, murmuring to Bwlch.

"Why couldn't I speak?" I demanded of Canyd. "He'll think it was my fault."

"Bericus won't. He knows ponies. He can also figger things out hisself, you know." And Canyd chuckled.

"How would he know it was Iswy did this?"

"How do you?" Canyd asked, his eyebrows reaching up his forehead into his thick white hair.

"I heard him. In the woods, asking Bericus to ride Cornix. But Bericus refused him. I heard Iswy cursing and promising that he'd get to ride the stallion one way or another. So he has lamed Spadix on purpose, so I can't lead Cornix. And no one can lead him from a mare. Nor the other stallions. Not Cornix."

"Aye, lad, you've the answer."

"And what about Spadix?" A sudden fear coursed through me. I almost wailed as I said, "We can't leave him behind."

"True."

"It'll be days before Spadix can walk! And Bericus won't wait on a pony!" I had never been so afraid for another living creature, not even during the roughest days crossing the Narrow Sea, when I had worried so about the foals.

"Now, lad"—and Canyd took my hand in a firm grip of gnarled fingers, waving the index finger of his other hand in my face—"how do you know what a great lord like Bericus will or will not do?" He straightened up. "There, an' I've never knowed the bran to fail me."

By the time Canyd and I had returned to the fire, Bericus had come to a decision.

"How long before the pony'll be sound, Canyd?" he asked.

"Two, three days. Ponies is tough."

Bericus sighed again. "Much as I hate to leave you, lad, we've got to move on today," he said, and I nodded, feeling a numbness; but I really did understand. "We'll leave you provisions and you can follow at your own pace. It's a good road all the way to Glevum from here. And you're sure to catch up with us before Bravonium, or by Virconium at the very latest." He put one hand on my shoulder and gave me an encouraging shake. "We must make good time while we have the weather."

"I understand, Lord Bericus."

Out of the corner of my eye, I saw Iswy's smug expression, and I drew in a deep breath to steady myself against the hatred I felt for him.

And so I had to watch as the camp was cleared, packs secured to the ponies, the mares and stallions bridled or haltered. I stood holding Spadix's lead rope. I tried not to look in Iswy's direction, not to see the triumph on his face when he was given the stallion to ride.

But it was Bericus himself who stood at the stallion's side for a leg up.

I held my breath, for although I knew that the Companion was a very good horseman, he was not the master that *Comes* Artos was. The stallion jibed under him, bucking in place at the unaccustomed weight on his back, snorting and arching his neck, trying to pull against the reins. Finally he moved out, still snorting and sidling. I really shouldn't have taken note of the apprehension on Bericus's face. Nor noticed the way Bericus tucked his long legs as tightly to the stallion's sides as he could. I think that was part of the trouble; the rider was saying "go" when he meant "no."

They had no sooner got to the head of the column than Cornix squealed, got his head down, and bucked. Three mighty heaves of his big frame, and Bericus was sprawled on the ground.

Someone tittered. Both Canyd and I looked in Iswy's direction but he had his head turned away.

Cornix did not run off, as everyone seemed to have expected; for immediately they had spread out to catch him. He trotted back the way he had just come, ears pricked, and then stopped to stretch his neck toward Spadix, beside me. He whuffled as if asking why Spadix was not moving out. I quietly caught the trailing reins.

Bericus was shaken by his fall; dusty but not hurt. There was a rueful expression on his face as he brushed himself off and came back for the stallion.

"Iswy!" he called, taking the stallion's reins from my hand, and I shivered with the unfairness by which Iswy had got the ride. "Let's see if you can stay astride. Unless anyone else wants to try?" And he grinned as he glanced about the circle of men.

"He won't stay up either," Canyd said in a low voice meant only for my hearing.

"He won't?"

Canyd chuckled and folded his arms across his chest. "Watch."

Boldly, and with a very smug smile on his face, Iswy ignored the helpful hand Bericus held out and, gathering the reins in one hand, vaulted neatly to the stallion's back. The stallion flicked his fine ears and shifted his feet, but he stood there. I groaned softly, disappointed in Cornix's loyalties. Decius brought up Bericus's customary mount and gave the Companion a leg up. I heard what could only have been a sigh of relief from the man, and then he gave the order to move out.

Iswy guided Cornix in behind Bericus's horse. As he did so, he shot a self-satisfied glance over his shoulder at me, standing by my poor lame pony.

He got no more than a few lengths from us when Cornix abruptly twisted, dropped his shoulder, and sent Iswy plowing his length in the dust. Canyd contented himself with a snort but I had to turn away so Iswy couldn't see the breadth of my smile.

The look on the Cornovian's face as he sprang up from the roadway was vicious. As he followed the stallion back to Spadix, I saw his hand go briefly to the slingshot looped over his belt.

"Easy now, lad," Canyd said to him in an urgent low tone, for Iswy had tried to grab the stallion's reins in a vindictive manner.

But Cornix could take care of himself, and he moved sideways—just as Iswy lunged for his reins a second time. Swift as a serpent, Iswy put his hand on a faggot of wood left for me by the fire, and he brandished it at the stallion, who merely flung up his head and backed.

Bericus caught the upheld wood from Iswy's hand and then flung it far away.

"If I ever see you . . ." Bericus's face tightened with anger. "Take the sack by Galwyn's feet and get on your way. You are dismissed from service."

"But—but—" Iswy protested, screwing his face up and dropping to one knee.

Canyd reached down for the sack and tossed it deftly to Iswy's bent figure.

Bericus swung his right leg over his stallion's back, dropping to the ground in a fluid movement. Grabbing Iswy up from the dust, he pushed the sack into his hands and spun him about, shoving him off in the direction we had come.

We all watched silently as Iswy, head bowed in dejection, walked slowly down the road. Once he turned, hand raised toward Bericus, hoping for a last-minute reprieve; but even Decius and Egdyl regarded him with hostility.

When the small figure had reached the roadway and disappeared from view, Bericus turned to the others.

"Set up the camp again," he said, heaving a gusty sigh.

I felt worse than ever and hung my head, but Canyd gave me a shake.

" 'Tis not you, lad, but that black devil who's called the turn of the die. I've seen it afore with highstrung animals." And he walked away, shaking his head at such whimsical behavior.

WE CHANGED THE POULTICE twice that day in the hopes of extracting the poisonous humors from Spadix's leg. I brought him the best grass I could find, and some clover for Cornix, which he liked especially. When no one was looking or in hearing distance, I stroked the stallion's neck and told him what a very clever, loyal friend he was.

Midafternoon, Bwlch burst back into camp, just ahead of a farmer and a heavy two-wheeled cart drawn by two stout ponies.

"We've only to get the pony into the cart—he'll fit, I know!" Bwlch exclaimed, his face flushed with delight in his solution. "And the farmer has agreed to take us down the road until Spadix can walk out himself."

The farmer seemed overwhelmed by all the excitement, open mouthed, digging the toes of his worn sandals into the dust. But when it came time to bargain for his services and the use of his cart and the ponies to draw it, he miraculously recovered his wits.

"For all I've to do at m'farm, an'none but me to do it, good lord . . ."

Bericus attempted not to look so pleased at this encouraging answer, and the bargaining lasted a long time, with me holding my breath for fear that the farmer would be too greedy, and for fear that any price would cost *Comes* Artos more than my pony was worth, even if Cornix would not move out of his company. Then hand smacked hand and the deal was concluded.

Fortunately the back of the cart could be removed and now formed a ramp, which Spadix gamely hobbled up in response to my ardent encouragement. He then looked around from his vantage point, in mild surprise to find himself on a level with the bigger horses. I had to perch on an uncomfortable corner of the cart, but Cornix led like a lamb, just as long as Spadix was nearby. We proceeded in this fashion for three days, until the swelling had subsided and Spadix was able to put his foot to the ground.

I don't know who was happier to see the last of the farmer and his heavy cart: myself, Bericus, or Spadix.

THE BEST PART OF those three days was Canyd's company, for the old hostler decided to ride with me. I believed I'd asked a simple question, like why Spadix's leg had swollen only to the knee, and I was suddenly being taught the construction of the leg and the hoof.

"Without a hoof, you've no horse, lad."

There was no longer any doubt in my mind that Lord Artos had been quoting old Canyd that night on the way to Burtigala.

"Care for their feet," he went on, "an' ease the tiredness of their legs, an' you've a horse to carry you. 'Tis the foot that carries the pony an' you."

I got interested, as much because it was a way of passing the slow hours of our marching as because I found that I wanted to know more. Old Solvin had said that horses would teach you something new every day of your life and you'd never get to know *all* there was to learn of them. If any came close to such total knowledge, it was surely Canyd.

Occasionally another rider would pass close enough to the cart to hear these lessons, and he'd roll his eyes sympathetically. But I did not for a moment consider Canyd Bawn's words boring.

That first evening, Canyd drew sketches in the dirt near the firelight, delineating the bones and tendons of a horse's leg.

"That's all they is, bone and tendon. For all it's the most important part of a horse, there's little flesh. Lose the foot and you've lost the horse."

I grinned at his repetition. He had a variety of phrases expressing the same truism. But I was also impressed by the masterful way his knifepoint depicted each separate part of the whole.

"When we get to the farm, I can show you. I've saved a leg and a hoof to illustrate what I mean." And now he laid a finger alongside his nose. "Like I thought, big horses like them 'uns are going to need special care. For their hooves. No hoof, no horse."

I grinned again but said I looked forward to seeing a leg and a hoof—though I didn't then realize what he meant.

We would all be glad to reach the end of this journey, for the weather had turned raw, with sleet showers more frequent, as well as frost liming the grass in the mornings.

Then, coming out of a fold of the hills, we could see the road running straight to the walled city of Deva.

"About a thousand souls or so," Bericus replied when I asked him how many lived there. I caught my breath at the thought of so many people living in one place, fortified against raiders as it was. "But we go east, to the farm"—and he pointed with his riding stick. "No need to go into the city at all."

I was disappointed not to have a chance to wander through a place of that size. I knew it had been a legionary fortress and its stout walls had been repaired many times.

"Don't worry, lad, you'll have a chance to see the city later," Bericus said to console my obvious chagrin. "If only to hear mass."

The Devan group among us now stretched their mounts' stride in an effort to reach home by darkness. Spadix could trot with the best of them, and all the Libyans seemed infected by the excitement of their riders.

WE ARRIVED AS DUSK was settling, but we had been seen on our approach through the lush pastures where cattle, ponies, and horses grazed. The geese who were penned during the day by the main gate honked and flapped their wings, telling all who hadn't heard that there were visitors. My father had also used those birds as nightly watchguards: I had scars on the calves of my legs to prove their diligence. Here there were also three big mastiffs, chained to the wall by day. These were let loose at night but knew who should and should not be about the enclosure at odd hours.

I was surprised by the extent of the farm, for the

main buildings, like the city, were stoutly walled against intruders. But then an establishment of its prestige would have to be secure from all but the most insistent attacks. Inside the thick walls there were many buildings, including a long low range of stables and barns, as well as cots for the farmworkers. The villa that would house *Comes* Artos on his visits was extensive, and it was several weeks before there was any occasion for me to enter it. On those rare occasions when I did enter, it reminded me too much of the home I had lost. My uncle had taught me well the humility required by my reduced state, and I would never forget those lessons.

THERE WERE HAPPY REUNIONS for the Devan riders, much time spent examining the fine Libyans by torchlight and lantern. I thought I was seeing double, for a man as like Canyd Bawn as two leaves of the same tree—save for having two sound shoulders—was weaving in and out, stroking each of the Libyans in turn, as if introducing himself to them. Having done so, he gave orders that the horses must be immediately settled. Then there would be time enough to exchange news and have the evening meal, which our coming had interrupted.

"Is he kin to you?" I had the chance to ask Canyd as I led Cornix and Spadix into the great barn.

"Own brother," Canyd said, his tone hovering between pride and irritation. "Rhodri. He trains the horses, while I keep them sound for him to do so."

I remembered then that Lord Artos had spoken of this Rhodri.

Cornix and the other three stallions were housed in their own barn, with the three pony stallions already standing at the stud.

"The stalls are big enough, lad," Canyd said, waving me to lead both stallion and pony inside. "Take whichever one on the left is free."

I had no sooner swatted Spadix on the rump to enter the stable—for where the pony led, the stallion would easily follow—then I heard a shout.

"What are you doing, idiot?" A dour-faced man rushed down the aisle toward me, brandishing his pronged wooden hay fork. "Such a spavined, ring-boned, misbegotten—"

"Not so fast, Teldys," Canyd said from the entrance. "Unless of course you want this fine new stall in splinters."

Teldys grounded his hay fork with a thump, looking from me to Cornix, who was now trying to pull free to join the pony in the stable.

"Ah! Like that, is it? And this is that so-special stallion Lord Artos bade me take extra care of?" His eyes wandered appraisingly over the black Libyan. "Well, I suppose we can see our way clear. Good job we made it larger'n usual. In you go with him, lad . . . What'd you say your name was?"

"He's Galwyn, pledged to be Artos's man," Canyd replied before I could open my mouth.

"Is he good enough for this black demon," Teldys asked, "since he and his pony know the beast so well?"

"Aye. You don't have to watch him to be sure he does what you tell him," Canyd said, nodding his head approvingly. "But see for yourself. Don't take my word for it."

"As if I'd ever argue with you, you old coper." And a smile lit the man's solemn features.

I came to learn that Teldys, who was Lord Artos's stallion man, actually had a merry temperament; it was just that the bones of his face were long and the flesh on them seemed to be pulled down to his jawline, giving him such a dour look. He had a quick infectious laugh that you couldn't help grinning at. And he listened. An admirable quality in anyone, as I discovered. I was quick to notice that no one argued with him and every one of the men moved hastily to perform the duties he assigned them.

"So, Galwyn, bed your charges down for the night, now we've finally got us all home where we belong." Canyd winked at me before he turned away to settle Paphin.

When all the horses had been properly bedded, we were taken into the farm kitchen and fed an excellent hot stew with fresh bread, which, I must say, I had missed on the road. And there were pears as well as apples to eat. Not much fresh fruit had come my way since my father had died.

I didn't mind that I was assigned a cot with the other unmarried men of the farm, and a peg for my scant clothing. The bedstead had a pallet of fresh straw and a good woolen blanket, and I could have slept anywhere that night and not heard the snores around me.

Thus began my service on Lord Artos's farm near Deva.

Part Three

deva

THOSE FIRST FEW WEEKS I couldn't have been happier in my new home. Though I was a stranger and this a closeknit group, I felt far more comfortable than I ever had on the *Corellia*. There were, of course, horses to talk about, and at our evening meal that first night Teldys wanted to hear all about our journey to Septimania and the horse fair. He seemed determined to draw every last word of description out of me: of the fair itself, the people and horses at it— every variety, including the black Libyans that Lord Artos had settled on as the proper steed. Teldys's wife, Daphne, wanted to know more about the outlandish things we had been given to eat. I talked myself hoarse and then realized that I had, and desperately hoped I hadn't made a bad impression on my very first day. But almost everyone had questions and certainly they listened without fidgeting. On our way to our quarters, I was teased, but not in a mean fashion—more as if they envied me the sights and marvels I had seen.

The routine of a horse farm is much the same everywhere, and I don't suppose it will change no matter who is *Comes*, prince, chieftain, consul, or even emperor. Horses must be fed and watered, their stables cleaned, and their bodies groomed and ridden, or themselves turned out to exercise in the fields. One falls into the rhythm of a pattern, so that day follows day and only the weather seems to change.

Except that roughly five weeks after we arrived at Deva, and for three days in a row, when I went to collect Spadix and Cornix from their field their coats were rough and sticky with sweat, as if they had been run hard. They had been the only two in their pasture, so they hadn't been competing. And besides, horses don't run themselves that hard, not ever. The second day, I spoke to Canyd about it and he checked both animals over, puzzled by their condition. He then discussed the matter with Teldys, and the head man was as bewildered as we were. The next morning I could not take offense when Teldys accompanied me as I walked the two out to their field. Before he let them loose, he went over them carefully, noting with a nod of his head that I had given them a good brushing off, which was my evening duty.

He also went with me at dusk to bring them in. Once again they showed signs of having sweated heavily.

"As if they had been galloped from here to Deva and back," Teldys said, gathering his heavy eyebrows in a frown.

"Or chased," I said, and looked beyond the hedges that separated the fields.

"A point you have there, lad," Teldys said with a heavy sigh, also casting his eyes around. "We shall set a watch, then, and see if we can catch whoever."

We caught no one at that field; I was the eyes that

were set to watch, secretly lodged in a tree bordering the field. But that evening, Splendora hobbled back from her pasture and instantly Canyd was called to see what had caused her lameness. I was grooming Cornix when Canyd called me to the door of the box stall. He said nothing as he opened his hand to show me a bloody thorn in his palm.

"Iswy's here?" I cried. My heart pounded so hard I was sure that it was audible to Canyd.

"A nasty streak that Iswy has in him, and he claiming to be a horseman!" Canyd snorted. "Some of those Cornovian tribesmen are like that. Take a real delight in avenging themselves for the silliest points of honor."

"But where's he staying?"

"Oh"—and Canyd threw up one hand, dismissing that consideration—"*that* one can live off the land. He's a dead shot with that sling of his. Or he's mixed in with some of those who roam these parts, picking up what they find whether it's theirs or no. Couple or three times, we've had to patrol the roads from Deva against bands of thieves. Like attracts like, you know." Then Canyd slapped my back in a friendly fashion. "The important thing is that your bay pony was too smart to be caught twice . . . and saved the stallion, too, I warrant."

"But I saw no one. No one in the field, nor in the roadway!" I cried, lest they think I had fallen asleep or been inattentive in my guarding.

"The mares're fields away from where you were, lad. No fault to you." Canyd patted my shoulder reassuringly.

"But Iswy's out there—" I began, distressed at the Cornovian's vindictiveness. Why should he take so against Cornix? No one else had been able to ride the stallion. Was Iswy that vain of his riding ability? But to avenge himself on a mare simply because I had ridden her now and then? Or was he avenging himself on all of us for his dismissal? Surely he had only been hired to journey with the horses to Deva. Had he expected to be taken on to work here? Or had Prince Cador dismissed him when he had returned? Such thoughts galloped about in my mind, but I spoke none of them aloud.

"We shall take precautions, never you fear, lad. Those animals be too valuable. Teldys will spread the word to watch for a lad of Iswy's description. He'll be sent about his business. You'll see."

"Splendora?" I asked as Canyd turned away.

"She's suffered no lasting harm. You're a good lad. Don't worry."

TELDYS SENT A MESSAGE to Bericus concerning the possibility of a band of marauders in the vicinity of the farm. For the next several weeks, we rode out in groups, exercising the Libyans in the fields nearest the buildings. Otherwise they were stable-bound, with the mastiffs and geese let loose in the farmyard to warn of intruders at night. And there were men working in every field, mending the hedgerows or doing other "repair" work. Not a meadow that didn't have some eyes on it every hour of the day.

One night the winds blew such a gale that, in the morning, thick frost rimed bare tree, hedge, and grass.

The day was bitterly cold and the footing so treacherous we turned no horse out. Three days the cold snap continued, and we had to break ice from the troughs and from the pond so the horses could drink.

Teldys and Canyd were of the opinion that, with cold winter blowing down over the land, we were unlikely to experience any more unwelcome attentions. I was not so sure: Iswy was sneaky as well as mean. The weather might have defeated him for now, but I intended to keep my eyes and ears open. None of Lord Artos's black Libyans would fall victim to his wickedness: this I swore to myself.

BY THE TIME THAT YEAR ended in the winter solstice and we at the farm had properly observed the birth of Jesus Christ, I learned the hard way that Canyd was the best bone setter as well as horse coper.

Rhodri required me to learn to ride well enough to handle any of the horses on the farm. And because the Libyans knew me, I had to ride them. I dislocated my shoulder twice falling off Splendora, who had healed sound after the thorn incident. Then I snapped the two bones in my left forearm when Spadix stumbled while we were rounding up the mares and foals prior to a storm. So that fall did what the now-absent Iswy had not—kept me off horses.

Canyd set the arm. His hands were as gentle on a human as on a horse, but I could do little with the splinted arm. Teldys assigned me to Canyd to do what I could, helping him prepare his herbs and simple remedies for equine ailments. Even with one hand, I could strip bark from river willows. And did—for days.

Unfortunately the injury also prevented me from attending mass at Christmastide in Deva. I sorely missed the joy of the Nativity mass, but only Teldys, Daphne, and their sons braved the wintry roads to make the journey. Still we made merry with the feast prepared by all the women on the farm. They had been cooking for days, each trying to outdo the others with soups, pies, and special dishes of quail, goose, and duck. There were also roast kid, roast suckling pig, venison, and vegetables, then all sorts of honey-sweet cakes, as well as all the frumenty we could eat. I enjoyed myself, though some of the older men drank too much mead and were very unwell the next day. I was determined to show my reliability in caring for Cornix, so I did not overindulge. Indeed, Canyd and I were the only ones sober enough to do the horses the next morning.

CANYD USED MY CONVALESCENT TIME to teach me more about The Hoof. From a shelf in his little cot, he brought down the bones of a horse's leg, with the dried tendons yellow against the dark ivory of the bone. He pointed out the small pastern bone, the navicular, which can easily be chipped enough to lame a horse so badly it has to be put down. The larger pastern bone was in place above them. I could actually move the knee and fetlock of this relic. He had dried out a hoof as well, the flesh carved out so I could see into the coronet band and the horny shell that protects the frog, the inside of it striated with fine vertical lines of hoofhorn. The hoofwall was actually no thicker than half the nail of my index finger.

"This is like your own finger- and toenails, Galwyn," Canyd explained, watching me examine the relic. "See here, where there are ridges? Bad year for this horse. See here, where there are cracks? He wasn't getting the right feed to keep his bones strong . . ."

He took the hoof in his hand, turning it around and around, obviously pondering some problem.

"Sorry, lad"—and he handed it back. "There is such a thin wall. One would have to be so careful . . ."

"Of what?" I prompted when the silence continued.

Canyd inhaled and then tapped the hoof. "You know, don't you, that all the Libyans are footsore—between hoof rot and cracks?"

I nodded, because it had been the talk of everyone in the cot: How was Lord Artos going to use horses who kept going lame? Ponies might not be big enough but they were sturdy and never had such problems with their feet.

"Those big Libyans have nice long hooves but they are accustomed to rocky and sandy surfaces. We have more bogs and marshes hereabouts, an' I mislike what the wetness does to these hooves, especially with such a high frog, where the mold likes to settle."

"But it's all hard," I said, tapping the shell. "Surely . . ."

"You've scrubbed stables down afore now, lad, and weren't your nails soft after a day in water?"

"Yes, they were—but they're only fingernails, not tough hoof like this."

"The pony that wore this foot was born and bred on this island. Big and strong as the Libyans are, they will need something to keep their feet up out of constant contact with wet ground. If we could only—" He broke off, frowning to try and catch some elusive notion. Then he reached into a dark corner and brought out some very odd looking pieces of leather. One had strings attached to it. He tapped the surface and I identified it as boiled leather, from which my father's guards had made their breastplates and the skirts that fell from waistline belts to protect their thighs from arrows.

"D'you know what this might be, lad?"

Some memory struggled to be recalled: something said in Lord Artos's voice.

"Look at it." And he pushed the thing into my hand. A rounded piece of boiled leather, all right, a sort of sandal—but for what sort of short and rounded foot . . . ?

"A sandal for a horse?" Yes, that was what Lord Artos had said of Canyd: He wanted to put sandals on horses to protect the hooves he was always talking about. I picked up the strings. "And these tie it on . . . ?"

"Good, lad! But leather, as tough as it can be made, is scraped and worn out in several days, and it takes weeks to prepare."

Then he handed me some flat metal crescents. They, too, had ties, but it didn't take me a minute to see that going over rough ground would split the thongs and the sandal would come off. Or it would hang by one tie and be a danger to the animal, not a protection.

"I think we may have to nail it to the hoof . . ."

I gasped, knowing very well how any sort of puncture in the foot could lame a horse.

"If"—and now Canyd's gnarled forefinger circled the rim of the hoof—"we very carefully put our nails into this part of the horn . . ."

I know I gawked my astonishment at him, and he smiled.

"Alun and I have been working—oh, years now, I think"—and he grinned at me for all that time spent on vain effort—"on the type of nail that would be slim enough to go in just this area and strong enough to hold a metal rim on the hoof. No hoof, no horse!"

"I know, I know."

"But the time has come, has it not, when those Libyans are goin' to need somethin' to protect 'em. Best we figure it out this time." He gave an emphatic nod of his head. "Had a pony once with bad cracks in his hooves. Fine pony, save for that, so Alun and me did keep the hoof from spreading with a metal rim . . . Should have kept on at the proper sort of sandal then." He frowned then and dismissed me to my evening chores.

It should not have surprised me that the next day I was ordered to Alun the Smith's forge, where he did all the metalwork required by the large farm, including making the flat spather swords used by the guards. Alun was the biggest man I had ever seen, with arms like tree trunks and a chest that was as deep and broad as Cornix's. He had a cap of very curly black hair, just grizzling above the ears, and a face with smears of soot generally on the ruddy cheeks. When he smiled, and he was a smiling man, he nearly lost his eyes in the creases of his flesh. He had four great anvils about his big fire, and three apprentices: two were his sons, built on the same generous lines as their father, and one a thinner lad who never smiled the whole time I lived at the Devan farm.

Alun and Canyd were working at one of the anvils in the forge, once again trying to find a shape of nail to suit the requirements. Round ones had long since been discarded as unsuitable, though I often heard Alun say that he forged the best nails from Venta to Eburacum. I was set to working the bellows, a job I could easily do with the one hand I had to work with. It was not an easy job, though, for the coal fire had to be very hot to heat the iron enough to make it malleable.

In that forge, I also saw the various shapes of horse sandals that had been devised over the years Alun and Canyd had been experimenting. Sandals with lips three-quarters of the way around that would be hammered down to fit tightly against the outside of the hoof; sandals with long clips that fit halfway up the outside of the hoof. Canyd thought that clamping the clip while still hot and malleable to the horse's hoof would seal it on. I fretted about red-hot iron being applied to a hoof, but Canyd and Alun laughed at my fears.

"There's no feeling to the outer shell. It's deader'n fingernails, you can be sure o' that," Alun told me. "But if it will save the hoof"—and he winked at me, jerking his head at Canyd to be sure I caught the jest—"then that one'll be happy, now, won't he?"

As Canyd laughed at such wit, I was able to smile back. Despite the heat and the smells in the forge—for

I was at the back of it, against the wall that ringed the home farm, and constantly inhaling the odd odors of hot metal and coal—I had a sense that these two men were on the brink of an extraordinary accomplishment.

"Light enough to be lifted, strong enough to protect, sturdy enough to last, and easy to place," I often heard Alun declare.

A flanged sandal was finally eliminated, though such a one stayed on an old pony for weeks. It had to be removed because the thick mud of the winter fields seeped in between hoof and metal, causing the old horse to go lame.

If I heard Canyd murmur, "No hoof, no horse," once, he said it like a litany as he and Alun attacked their objective. And I got so I would groan in protest the moment he formed the first "No."

AS THE WEATHER IMPROVED and spring seemed nearer, I hoped in vain that Lord Artos would come to inspect his mares and foals. Bericus came every month, checking each of the twenty Libyans and the foals himself, though he also read Teldys's laboriously written daily reports. Bericus would ride into the yard on the heavy-boned bay gelding that took him on all his travels, for the horse farm was not the only property Lord Artos had in this area. He would bellow my name and bring me running.

"You get taller every time I see you, lad," Bericus would say.

In truth I *was* getting some growth, with all the good food Daphne liked to set upon her table. We even had meat twice a week.

Then Bericus would toss me the reins of the gelding and turn to have a few words with Teldys while I stabled the horse.

"Has Cornix eaten the pony yet?" Bericus might ask as we three strode down to the stables. Lord Artos's stallion was always the first to be seen on these inspection visits.

I'd have to strip the rug off Cornix—which I did even with my broken arm—for Bericus was thorough. He'd run his hands down each leg to assure himself of soundness, and pat the smooth hide. And after the first time Cornix got hoof rot, Bericus always checked each foot. I was careful to use a powder to prevent it, so he never found another trace of it.

"How long d'you think it'll take before they grow their own winter coats, Teldys?" Bericus asked. "Won't be able to pamper them on the march."

"A year or two," Teldys said. "They have to adapt. Horses do."

Then Spadix would nose Bericus for the turnip or parsnip that he always seemed to have in his belt pouch.

"Beggar," Bericus said, but he provided the treat while Teldys tutted in disapproval. "How's the arm, Galwyn?" He'd teased me the first time he'd seen it splinted.

"Itches something fierce," I said, but showed him the smooth willow wand that was long enough to help relieve the itching. "Canyd says it'll mend straight," I added, in case Bericus might think I couldn't do right by Cornix.

"Good bones, the lad has," Teldys said, giving me an affectionate buffet on my good shoulder.

If Bericus had time to spare, he would take a meal with Teldys, where doubtless they discussed other matters. Then he would ask me to saddle up the gelding, and while I did that—awkwardly with the broken arm, but refusing his help—Bericus would often tell me more about Lord Artos's activities.

"You see, it's not just the horses the *Comes* needs, Galwyn. It's the support of other princes around about us here," Bericus said. "Most of them haven't seen these fine Libyans yet, of course, so they have doubts about the effectiveness of Artos's plans to defeat the Saxons the next time they're on the move."

"But surely Lord Artos only has to *tell* them . . ."

Bericus laughed. "He's a grand one for talking, and while he's with them, they're all for him. He's got a way of making men loyal to him." He looked at me and smiled again. "Of course, the Companions, myself included, are still the only ones who really understand the merits of his great plan to unite all Britons against the Saxons."

"But—but—" I spluttered, wondering how anyone could listen to Lord Artos and *not* believe in his strategies.

"It's the doubters that must still be convinced—against their will, lad. That's why politics is so important," Bericus replied with a grin, clapping his hand on my shoulder; and then, unexpectedly, he peered at me. "I do believe you've put a full hand in height on you since you came back from Burtigala . . ." He paused, stepping back to arm's length, to study me. "Aye, and muscled up, too." And he squeezed the shoulder I had dislocated twice.

"I'm helping Canyd and Alun," I said, rather proudly.

"No better men to have as exemplars," he agreed, nodding. "Now politics is how Artos is contriving to keep the kingdom quiet until he is ready to exhibit his new force. You do all you can"—and again he pressed my shoulder—"to further that, and you'll have the full gratitude of the *Comes—and*"—he grinned again—"the profound thanks of all of us who will ride to battle on our fine black horses."

Bericus swung up into the saddle. "One day, when spring is finally here"—and he wound his cloak tightly about him—"you may have a chance to see our new headquarters. It's slow work but it'll be a fine place when it's finished: a base for our cavalry and a place for training the foot soldiers." He looked off, frowning slightly. "The Saxons remain where they are. It's the Irish we have to contend with right now. *Vale*, Galwyn," he said in farewell as he kneed the gelding forward. "Just keep the Libyans safe and prospering!" he cried over his shoulder.

As if he needed to tell me. I thought constantly about their safety, Iswy topmost in my mind. Not that we had seen hide or hair of Iswy after that heavy frost. Nor had there been any roving bands stealing from outlying farms or harrying travelers on the roads. Still, I never forgot that particular danger.

I knew about the danger of Irish raiders, too, living as we did not that far from a favorite landfall of theirs. No wonder princes and chiefs around here were not quite so concerned about Saxon invasions, despite the well-founded rumors that Aelle and his sons intended to expand beyond their pale near Eburacum. The Irish were a problem *now*; the Saxons only a distant menace.

Of course, for Lord Artos's marvelous plan of a swift-moving force to succeed, it would be five or six years before this year's crop of foals were ready for battle. Would we be given the time? Would enough of the princes join forces with Artos to provide a large enough army?

In point of fact, the Libyan stallions could have been used in battle right now, since Rhodri had trained them to respond to movements of heel and seat so that a Companion had both hands free for his weapons. And I had to admit I dreaded the day Cornix would be taken from my care, for he was, indeed, the mark of both *Comes* Artos's favor and my status on the farm.

BERICUS WAS NOT the only one who noticed that I had grown taller and stronger. All those hours on the bellows and the generous, good food were having an effect. Further, now that my arm bones had knit, I was excused from pumping the bellows and allowed to help make the horse sandals, which meant much work with a hammer.

Bericus had listened to both Alun and Canyd explaining about their device: had listened but had not seemed terribly impressed.

"He only *rides* the horses," Canyd said later, when Alun had railed against Bericus's lack of enthusiasm. "He hasn't the care of them."

"He cared for them on the journey here," I said.

Canyd eyed me a moment. "For his own, but not for all the others who are in our keeping."

"Aye, he's a Companion," Alun said, altering his position, but I don't think it was out of deference to my remark. The smith enjoyed opposing Canyd, if only to be contrary. But it was a good-humored antagonism.

That might even have been what led to an effective horse sandal, because if Canyd suggested one method, Alun would counter with another, totally different. Thus they explored many more possibilities. Boiled leather had long been ruled out as ineffective, and now all their efforts were concentrated on developing an iron rim to somehow attach to the underside of the hoof.

Once again an older pony was used to test the result.

I do remember the look on the pony's face when he first realized he had something stuck to his hooves. He kept picking up his hinds and trying to kick off the unaccustomed weight. We had a good laugh at his antics.

I trotted him out into the cold wet afternoon, he still trying to dislodge the rims and then shying when the iron sandals clanged on stone. He picked his old legs up like a yearling, flicking his front feet. Gradually his kickings subsided as he realized he could not relieve himself of the encumbrances.

He was turned out again and was watched over the next few days, to be sure the metal plates did not cause lameness or, far more importantly, come off. The fifth day, a hind sandal did get sucked off by the thick mud in the pasture from the heavy spring rains.

Canyd and Alun passed the lost rim back and forth, noting the way that three of the five nails had come out and were sticking out of the rim. We found the other two in the pony's foot: they had broken off, but—and this was important—they had not made him lame by remaining.

"They don't sit in firmly enough, though, even with the tapering," Alun said, holding the erring nail up between thumb and index finger.

"But the other rims stayed on," I reminded them. "Three out of four is good."

"Aye," Canyd said, "for want of the right nail, the sandal was lost . . . and so would the horse be."

"Maybe"—and Alun pondered this before he spoke again, "maybe—if the nail is turned down—hooked, so to speak—on the outside, it will not pull out as easily."

"Aye, that would clinch it in place," Canyd agreed, nodding.

"I will make the nail a little longer, then," Alun said, motioning me to take my position at the bellows to heat up the fire, "to be hammered down on the hoof. It wouldn't hurt the animal, would it?"

Canyd shook his head.

THIS TIME THE SANDALS remained on a full two weeks.

"Problem with all these sandals and nails," Alun said when Canyd and I were jubilant to see success, "is that the hoof of a horse grows, or he rubs the sandal

113

on hard ground and gradually wears the nailhead down . . . or gets grit between hoof and sandal . . . or . . ."

"You've to train men to make the rims," Canyd said thoughtfully. "You've enough work on your hands just making arms an' tools. A man'd have to be sent along with the horses, an' with plenty o' nails, I 'spect, in case a shoe came loose or got lost." His wink at me was significant.

I stared back at him aghast, silently turning my thumb in my own direction.

"And why *not* you, lad?" Canyd went on. "You've been in on the work since it started." Then he added slyly, " 'Tis one way to get to be with *Comes* Artos, isn't it?"

I know I must have flushed to realize that Canyd knew of my devotion. But that remark settled my future. I was only glad that Alun agreed, grinning at me with his eyes so lost in the folds of his cheek flesh that only a twinkle remained.

"But . . . but . . . you've sons . . ." I began in humble protest. Even if their suggestion was my dearest wish come true, I was surely not the one to be chosen. "And Ratan, your apprentice—"

"None of whom can ride well enough to move with an army, lad," Alun said. "And I'd need them *here*." He gestured around the forge, with its buckets of arrowheads waiting to go to the fletcher, and lanceheads, and all the farm paraphernalia. "To do what they've been trained up to do." He nodded emphatically.

"Still an' all, you'll have to train up other lads, like

114

our Galwyn here, to know how to make the horse sandals," Canyd said.

"Aye, I will, won't I? But"—and now Alun pointed
his thick burn-scarred finger at me—"you'll need to
know more than just how to make the sandals. That's
only part of the whole."

"Aye, ye'll need to know the foot of a horse, and the
leg, and what can go wrong with both. No hoof, no
horse."

I rolled my eyes at Canyd for that but he, too, wag-
gled a forefinger at me.

"I know more ways to ease a lameness than stooping
legs in water, m'lad, and you'll have to learn 'em all."

That very day at the evening meal, they approached
Teldys, with me in reluctant tow, and asked to have
me assigned to them for teaching. Teldys had, of
course, been apprised of all their efforts to make a
horse sandal, and he even came to inspect the pony
who wore the first sets.

"You'll be wanting even more iron, then, won't
you?" he said with a sigh of resignation. "D'you know
how much it costs these days?"

"Any that's spoiled in practice can be melted down
and used again," Alun blithely assured him.

A CARTER CAME ONTO the farm one day, bearing
a message for me from my mother. It had been
written before the winter solstice and was a list of her
present dissatisfactions, including the fact that my
sister Flora had been married and I hadn't come to be
witness.

115

Salutations to Galwyn Gaius Varianus from his grieving mother, Serena, widow of Decitus Varianus, who is in good health despite her condition and who hopes to find you well.

Have you forgotten how to write and read so that you do not answer my last letter and give us no word of you since the scrawl that the carter brought us? You should have paid more attention to your tutors when you still had them. But there are others, surely, there in the north where you say you went, who are able to read and could have written on your behalf. Your sisters have persuaded me, against my better judgment, that it is possible that you were unable to convince your employers to let you come to your sister Flora's nuptials.

As this was the first letter I had received from anyone, I had to assume that a previous letter, containing the news of Flora's imminent wedding, had not reached me. How like my mother to think I could have forgotten how to read and write!

Lavinia insists that you were unable to come—rather than too lazy to make the journey. But surely you know that it would have been your duty to give your sister's hand, as you are the legal guardian of both sisters, though I know you are fonder of Lavinia than Flora but she is the elder and deserves your courtesy. You could at least have answered my letter.

Had you not left the employ of your uncle Gralior you would have been given leave to attend a family function. Indeed, he was here where you were not, and still displeased that you left his employ so precipitously. I thought you had been raised with more attention to courtesies and I cannot understand why you would distress your uncle who had great hopes for you in his business.

That was certainly the first I had heard of his hopes for me.

We are well enough here, though the winter was cold and I suffered from it badly with my feet and hands swollen with the chilblains you know I always have when I have to bide in an unheated place like this poor little house I must now occupy.

I am surprised, too, that you have made no attempt to see your family since your father's unfortunate demise. At least for the Winter Solstice, when it is the habit for families to come together. Not that we had much of a celebration but as much as I could manage. You would have been comfortable enough in the shed but it was most unkind of you not to come to Flora's wedding. She and Lavinia cried over your absence but I told them what could they expect of a boy who would leave a good position to go the gods knew where with strangers.

I close this now. Vale, your grieving mother.

The letter was both infuriating and depressing. It was true that Lavinia and I had always been the best of friends, but I would certainly have been happy to have attended Flora's wedding, to see her happy. Even if it had meant being in Uncle Gralior's company.

Obviously he had filled my mother's head with nonsense. "Hopes for my future" indeed! I was a lot better off with strangers than I had been on my uncle's ship.

I moped over her unkind words and accusations. Begging a piece of vellum from Teldys, I started to compose an appropriate response, not quite denouncing Gralior for the mean and brutal man he was but making it plain to her that I was in a much better situation in Lord Artos's service.

Teldys watched me struggling with the letter each evening and finally leaned toward me across the table.

"To your mother, is it?" And when I nodded, he added, "Sometimes these explanations are best made in person. There are those four horses Rhodri's been training for Prince Cador. You go with them and make it all right with your mother. She's at Ide, is she not? That's not far out of the way."

I was very grateful, for I would never have asked for such a favor. And so I went off with Firkin and Yayin to lead the horses. Yayin also had a personal problem this visit would solve: a chance to see his father, who had suffered a bad sword wound.

We delivered the horses and agreed to meet up on the road back to Deva the next day. Firkin went with Yayin.

MOTHER HAD TAKEN a second husband, a nice-enough man, a combmaker who was so skilled that people sent for combs of his making from as far away as Londinium.

His two-roomed cottage, close up against the walls of the old fort, was snug if certainly not what my mother had had when my father was alive. Odran had made every effort to improve the place and had even managed to have water from the old Legion aqueduct piped to a cistern just outside the door, so Mother did not have far to go to fetch the household water.

I was both disappointed and gratified that my mother didn't immediately recognize me. It was my younger sister, Lavinia, who shrieked in welcome and rushed into my arms to weep all over my chest.

"Galwyn, Galwyn, it is you!" Vinny exclaimed over and over. "Mother, it is truly Galwyn! Don't you know your own son?"

Mother blinked rapidly at me and it was not the first time that I thought my mother did not see well beyond the tip of her nose.

"Well, you certainly took your time making your way here," she said, folding her hands across her waist as if she did not wish me to see that she was plumper now. "Your uncle was terribly upset. At first he thought you had drowned at Burtigala and no one had bothered to tell him."

"But didn't my message reach you?" I asked, though I did not think she had grieved for me.

It was Lavinia who sniffed again. "Gill the carter brought it but it didn't arrive until weeks after you gave it to him. But we were so relieved, weren't we, Mother? Did you get ours about Flora's marriage?"

"I got that one only eight days ago."

Mother sniffed. "I paid good coin to be sure it reached you in time."

"I'm sorry, Mother, but it didn't. I came as soon as I

could. We had to deliver some horses to Prince Cador."

"Prince Cador, is it?" She sniffed again. "And Lord Artos. No wonder my sister's husband wasn't good enough for the likes of you."

"Oh, Mother, you just won't admit that Uncle Gralior is a mean, nasty man," Vinny said, shooting me a glance of encouragement. "Even when your own sister tells you the truth."

Mother made a sound that was so close to Spadix's snort of disgust that I had to cough suddenly.

"Oh, you must be thirsty," Vinny said anxiously.

"Come, we've small beer and a fine soup that Lavinia has made us," Odran said, gesturing for me to settle myself on the bench. "You can stop long enough for that, can't you?"

"I've only a few hours to spare," I said, which was not the truth; but Mother was scarcely welcoming.

"A few hours!" my mother said scoffingly. "And it's years since we've seen you."

"That's because Uncle Gralior would never give him enough time to visit us, Mother," Lavinia said with pointed sweetness. "I'll just slip around and tell Flora that you're here. She worried about you, too, Galwyn."

I loosened the girth of the pony I was riding, wishing that it could have been one of the Libyans, to prove to my mother that I was in far better service now than with that wretched uncle of mine.

Flora, well married and with a child under her apron, wept with joy at seeing me and dragged forward her husband, the local butcher, who had supplied the meat for the stew we then ate.

When I realized how eager my sisters were to know all about my recent adventures, I was quite willing to talk. And when I noticed that both Odran and Melwas, Flora's husband, were listening as avidly, I relaxed and began to enjoy myself.

For all her disclaimers, my mother indulged in few of her disparaging sniffs until I mentioned my work with Canyd and Alun.

"It is as well that your father is not here to listen to you prating about smithing." And she made her disdain obvious by looking down her nose at me.

"It is an honest trade," Odran said quickly. "You know how well Ide's smith lives."

That silenced her, but I had had enough. The meal was ended and I could take my leave without giving offense to anyone. I said all that was polite to Melwas and Flora, slipping to her the last of my gold rings as a wedding gift. Then I had to promise Lavinia faithfully that I would return whenever I could.

"I don't care what Mother says," Vinny murmured as I tightened my pony's girth. "I think your work sounds fascinating, and you were always fond of horses. And that's proper enough for a Varianus. Do come back anytime you can, Galwyn," she added so plaintively that I hugged her tightly and repeated my promise.

"I can't say when, of course, Vinny—"

"I know . . ." she said, her voice trailing off unhappily, but she was all smiles again when I turned back to give her a final wave.

Yayin was all smiles, too, when he and Firkin arrived at our meeting place. His father was recovering, if slowly. I think he had had the better visit. But we all traveled back with lighter hearts.

NOT A WEEK LATER, I found that I was to start my new profession far sooner than was planned; for just as spring was brightening the grassy meadows and I was coming to grips with the intricacies of my special training with both Canyd and Alun, a message came from *Comes* Artos. He wanted all four stallions to be brought to him as quickly as possible at Camelot, which was what he had named his new headquarters. He wanted to show the quality of the stallions to those who doubted their use in his strategy.

"It says here he's sending a troop to escort the stallions and whatever of the larger mounts Rhodri may have trained and ready. And see here, you're to come." Teldys's thick forefinger tapped at the paragraph. " 'The pony and his rider must come, too, if Cornix will not travel without their company.' "

Being sent from Deva also took care of my recurring nightmare: that Iswy would return to harass the Libyans once again, now that the weather was more clement. Then, of course, since I was such a worrier, I wondered if he would learn that the stallions had gone to Camelot and seek them out there.

"Bericus will be leading the troop?" I asked.

"Not likely," Teldys replied. "Don't you remember his last message? That he'll be away this month on service with Prince Cador? The Irish are raiding again."

I had forgotten and, for one moment, was downcast. I had hoped to have the support of Bericus both on the way and in Camelot.

"But . . . but . . ."

"But, but, but," Alun mocked me, smiling to show how pleased he was for my sake, "you'll do well enough."

"But if a horse should lose a sandal . . ." I protested.

"Who better than you to nail it back on?" Alun clapped me so stoutly that I staggered off balance, while Canyd smoothly caught my arm to restore my footing. "In truth, who else can we send? And you'll know what to do."

"But . . . but . . ." I was aghast at such responsibility. It would be my task to see that the priceless stallions arrived sound as well as safe. What if something happened to one of them, despite every precaution I could take?

Teldys held up his hand. "If Alun and Canyd say you're the one to go, you are."

I stopped protesting then. Because even I had to admit that I'd had more training than any of the others, no matter how inadequate I felt myself to be. Still, I was in a state of considerable apprehension, my mind continuing to dredge up, in increasingly horrific variety, all the disasters and accidents to which horses are prone.

Mind you, while they were readying the stallions and the pack animals for the journey, Canyd and Alun added to my apprehensions, battering me with *ifs* and *when*s and circumstances and how to repair hooves and which remedies to use for what travel problem.

Then, to my total consternation, Rhodri told me this time I would ride Cornix and lead the pony.

"You're far too heavy now to ride that pony such a

distance. And with his short legs, he'd be holding the cavalry to his pace. Not wise," Rhodri said. "Since he's still the stallion's stablemate, he must go, or unsettle Lord Artos's pride and joy. No, you lead him this time."

I was aghast. My ability to stay on a horse had improved, my reflexes sharpened by the desire to avoid more broken bones. And it was true that I had ridden Cornix from time to time and he seemed to be less fractious with me astride him than others.

"But ... but ..." Why was I putting up so many objections to having my most private dreams come true: to ride Cornix to Camelot; to see Lord Artos again; to be able to prove how useful I could be to him?

My thoughts were interrupted by a dig in the ribs from the mischievous Yayin, one of the unlucky riders who'd been thrown when trying to school the stallion. "And haven't you always been whispering in that pony's ear to tell Cornix to treat you nice?"

"I never—!" I turned on Yayin in self-defense. He jumped backward, grinning, and I realized he was only joking so I managed to laugh.

"Naw," said Firkin, "he just smears his saddlecloth with that smelly glue."

"That stallion knows just how much he can get away with, with Galwyn up," another suggested slyly.

"Not when I'm teaching him, he doesn't," Rhodri said sternly, and the lads pretended to cower before the trainer's displeasure. Then Rhodri put a companionable arm about my shoulders. "The horse trusts you, as you've had the care of him. I'd rather have someone he knows on his back for the journey than any stranger."

Once back at the soothing task of grooming Cornix while he stood, hipshot, eyes closed, enjoying the attention, I quite liked the notion of riding the great stallion all the way to Camelot. I'd grown not only taller but longer and stronger in leg and arm, so I really could control Cornix's explosive habits—most times. I knew he liked me, for he would come to his stall door on hearing my voice, and whicker at my approach. It was comical to see Spadix, who still shared the black's stall, push his nose up beside Cornix, trying to look out over the high stall door. I always greeted my faithful pony first, for he had, in his own small way, been one of the reasons I was here with the horses of the land, and not struggling with the horses of the sea.

However, I was the only one from the farm selected for the journey to Camelot. I was very proud of that, and then was beset with all kinds of conflicting emotions: I wasn't worthy of such trust; would I be able to cope with the responsibility? Would I know how to act at Camelot amidst warriors chosen for their skills, when I had only a small boy's knowledge of arms, and little training as a swordsman?

No one seemed at all surprised that I had been chosen. Indeed Yayin appeared more respectful and even Firkin deferred to me. That was embarrassing. We were all the same here at the farm, weren't we? We all mucked out every day, and exercised horses, and ate and slept together. I wasn't sure *which* disconcerted me most: being chosen, going, or the responsibility of riding Cornix there.

Before the escorting troop arrived, Daphne took a hand in outfitting me for journey. Inspecting my clothing, she found what I had in deplorable condition, despite my best efforts to keep my garments clean and mended. Riding horses in all sorts of weather does tend to wreak damage on clothing.

So I was clothed in new leggings and smocks for the trip, and given a fine tunic and colored leggings to wear for attendance upon Lord Artos.

"If I learn"—and Daphne shook her finger at me as she, almost reluctantly, handed over the finery, as well as the set of sturdier garments for travel—"that you have ridden in that good tunic, or worn it mucking out after that great black hulk, I'll flay you alive."

What delighted me most were the pair of fleece-lined boots that tied on all the way to my knees. These would help my shins and toes recover from the chilblains that often kept me awake at night. We were having a very cold spring and the itching kept me up, even with the salve Canyd had given me. Everyone was looking forward to warmer weather, when such winter ailments would cease.

THE TROOP ARRIVED—somewhat supercilious, as warriors can be, toward the farmers whom they protected. But the soldiers' attitude changed for the better when they saw the big, bold black Libyan stallions they must escort. The soldiers were properly impressed when they were taken to the fields to see the broodmares and their foals. The foals that they had had at foot last year were yearlings now, and if their glossy black-and-brown coats did not make them stand out from the native ponies, their size did. They were the same height as most of the grown animals at grass.

The captain of the troop, Manob, looked askance at me when I was introduced as Cornix's hostler and veterinary; he nodded more approvingly when Teldys listed my abilities.

Manob's men were a very rough lot and regarded mere farmers with small tolerance and much skepticism. I knew that I would have to prove myself to them on the trip and I was very nervous about that.

In my eyes, however, Manob rose in estimation when he most courteously asked Canyd to check over the feet of the troop's horses.

"Some need their hooves trimmed, and we've one that's walking short." Manob frowned. "But there's no heat in the leg."

"Bring him first," Canyd said, and gestured to me to accompany him.

Immediately Manob bellowed for the trooper to present his mount. Hoping I'd be able to guess right on the cause of lameness, I followed Canyd to the smithy. There we donned the heavy leather aprons that protected us against a horse pulling his foot roughly from our grasp.

I nodded at Alun and his sons, who were finishing the last of the sandals I would be taking with me. The day before, I had sharpened my hoof knives, so my tools were all in the smithy; but I didn't move for them until Canyd gave me another peremptory gesture. When he saw my startled expression, he nodded solemnly.

"Begin this journey as you mean to go on,

Galwyn," he said. The use of my name warned me that I would be doing the work while he oversaw it. Well, at least he'd be there now to support—or deny—my ministrations.

"Trot him up," Canyd called, waving his arm at the soldier leading a bright bay pony.

It, too, was larger than the usual moor ponies, and it occurred to me that Lord Artos had been trying before, with some degree of success, to breed size from local animals. But they were still ponies in build: stocky, short-coupled—tough, yes, but not long enough in the leg or big enough in the barrel and chest to support men who were seventeen or sometimes eighteen hands in height.

As I had been taught, I watched for any unevenness of stride.

"He's favoring the near fore," I said, noting when the pony's head bobbed.

Canyd made one of his agreeing sounds.

Even as we watched, the horse's stride leveled. When his rider brought him to a halt in front of us, I had a notion as to the problem.

Running my hand from the pony's shoulder down his leg, I could feel no heat. So I hauled his foot up by the hairy tuft of fetlock. He was, at least, well accustomed to having his feet attended, for he did not resist.

There was just a touch of heat in the sole, at one side. I took my tongs and clamped about that section of the horny hoof. The pony struggled to free his foot but I had it firmly caught between my knees and had set myself, prepared to forestall any resistance. I took a paring knife and carefully, right at the point of tenderness, cut. Almost instantly a gout of dirty gray-yellow fluid gushed out, released by the knife cut.

"What was that?" Manob asked, bending down to observe my handiwork.

"An old puncture wound grown over," I said in exactly the same level tone Canyd used when his guesses were correct. I turned to the rider. "Happens frequently, traveling rough country, no matter how careful you are of their feet. No hoof, no horse."

Canyd cleared his throat but I didn't look at him.

"Soak the foot for half an hour in warm water with a handful of salts in it. Then come back and we'll see if it's all clear."

"Yes, but can he be ridden?" The man evidently did not wish to be parted from his troop.

'He'll be fine. I've something to plug the hole with, a tar-soaked flax that'll keep it clean as well as aid in healing."

After that, Manob regarded me more favorably. I inspected forty-four hooves that afternoon, and trimmed dead horn from most of them, certain that they would leave the farm sound. Fortunately there was only the one lame pony in the troop.

IT WAS WHEN CORNIX was taken to water that evening that the soldiers discovered the sandals. The sound they made on the flags of the courtyard turned every head. Cornix was accustomed to his sandals by now and no longer lifted his feet or tried to kick the iron off his feet.

"By Mithras, what's wrong with that horse?" Manob cried.

"He has horse sandals on," Canyd said. "Made of iron. Needs to be so shod on the wet ground, and the sandals will prove useful in battle as well."

"Sandals for a horse?" Manob stared, round eyed with amusement. Then he guffawed. His men relaxed and grinned, taking their lead from their captain.

"Aye," Canyd said, nodding imperturbably. "Can't get no thorns or punctures through iron."

The captain's expression altered to a thoughtful one. Then he dismissed the matter with a shrug. "Doesn't happen that often."

"Often enough to leave you short of a man or two, I don't doubt," Alun said. "No hoof, no horse."

"They all done like that?" Manob asked.

Canyd nodded.

"They nailed on?" Manob was quick witted.

"And placed on the hoof hot, for the best fit," Canyd admitted blandly.

"Horse lets you?"

"Hmmm. They know what's good for 'em," Canyd said, giving the animals more credit for sense than humans.

"What happens if one does come off on the journey?"

"That's why Galwyn goes with you," Canyd said, delighting in the expression on the captain's face.

"He made the horse sandals?" Manob regarded me skeptically.

I knew I looked young, for I hadn't much in the way of face hair yet, but he didn't have to regard me as one would a child not yet out of leading strings.

"Indeed, he's right handy with hammer and tongs," Canyd said, in a sort of oblique warning.

"Seems to be," Manob remarked.

Part Four

CAMELOT

THE NEXT MORNING, when dawn was breaking, we left the farm at Deva, a cavalcade: myself astride Cornix, with Spadix on a lead rope beside us, and Manob on his gray stallion heading the troop. Under bridle, the two stud horses were very well mannered. The other three Libyans were led in the center of the troop.

We made good time that first day, though Spadix had to pump his legs hard to keep up with his friend; still he was tireless even at the canter. So he wouldn't feel worthless, I had him carry my pack of sandals and tools.

We had some days to travel, but we made far better progress than on my journey from Isca. We camped out, for the spring was warming, and Manob preferred camping to the rough inns available on this route.

"I can guard us better on our own. We know who is near and who should not be."

He was a good commander and we ate well, from what was hunted. He did buy bread when we passed villages that had bakers. It was rough bread, but great for soaking up the juices of the stews.

Although every day I mentally reviewed all the

things that could go wrong with hooves, none of them occurred on our journey. For the most part, we were traveling on good Roman-built roads. I checked the sandals morning and night, and the nails stayed firm. There was no sign of hoof rot. Manob usually managed to observe this procedure but said little. He did admire the little iron pick I had made to ferret stones and gravel out of the deep frogs. I had a few extras—for they are troublesome objects at times, forever getting lost in the straw—and gave him one.

Spring is always a good time to travel: the weather not too cold for comfortable riding nor the nights too chill to find sleep. Fields were greening with winter-sown crops and there was fresh grass for the horses to graze at night when they were picketed. The blossoming trees, pear and apple, were lovely, and the woods through which we traveled were bursting with buds, bluebells and daisies dotting the ground beneath us. Had I not been so anxious that nothing should go wrong on this journey, I would have enjoyed it even more.

I shall never forget my first sight of the hill on which Lord Artos had built his headquarters, Camelot. It rose out of the ground suddenly, as if a giant's fist had punched up just that much of the earth's surface to form it. The sides were, naturally, cleared of any vegetation, and we could see the course of the zigzag road that led up to the southwest gate, a massive affair of oak planks the width of a man's thigh. Sentries patrolled the top and the wooden palisade that surrounded it, for not all the walls were finished. Of course our approach was noticed and news of our arrival spread.

I was amazed to see horses tearing at breakneck speed down the approach road toward us, weaving through the obstacles of people, laden ponies, and ox-drawn carts. I wondered if they thought our troop was hostile, though everyone knew that the Saxons did not ride, nor had they horses of this quality.

And then—when they got closer—I saw it was Lord Artos himself who led the horsemen, his face broad with smiles, his bright hair golden in the sunlight.

"Galwyn! I wouldn't know you, lad, you've grown so. And able to ride my fine fellow, too."

If his words to me were welcoming, his eyes gleamed as they fell on the big stallion that Manob had assigned to the front of the troop.

He threw his gray's reins to one of his escort, swung lithely to the ground, and beamed up at me where I had halted his stallion. He put one hand proprietarily on Cornix's bridle.

"Rhodri's doing, my lord," I said, grinning from ear to ear. I immediately slipped my feet out of the foot plates and my right leg over the back of Cornix, dropping to the ground.

Well, I would never match Lord Artos in height or girth, but I didn't have to look up as far to meet his blue eyes now. And I had brought his fine stallions safely to him. With a bow of satisfaction at that accomplishment, I passed Cornix's reins to his rightful rider.

Lord Artos took them with a grateful smile, and

before I could clasp my hands together to offer him a leg up, he had vaulted to Cornix's back.

"Take my horse, Galwyn! Manob, my greetings, and thanks for the safe conduct. Can you help exchange saddles here? Cei, Geraint, Gwalchmei," he said to those who had ridden down with him, "you shall have the pleasure of riding my black horses back to Camelot. I'm eager for your opinion."

The change of saddles was accomplished with alacrity and gave the *Comes* a chance to try out the war training Rhodri had given Cornix, making the stallion walk from side to side and turn on the forehand, then turn on the hindquarters, all of which Cornix did smoothly. I would remember to tell Rhodri how wide Lord Artos smiled in the testing. Then Lord Artos gave the signal, and as the gray spurted forward instantly with the others, I found myself still in the van as we rode—not quite so furiously—up the road to Camelot.

How they had made it safely down the road at the pace they had come was beyond my understanding. Despite occasional loads of sand and pebbles to improve the footing and provide traction for the heavy carts, the roadway was slippery with mud. We had to thread our way past men and supplies of all sorts. Two of the Libyans, and even some of the troopers' mounts, shied when going by noisy, squeaking, heavy-wheeled drays that were bringing stone, timber, slates, and bricks up the steep and zigzagging slope.

We rode through the great wooden gates. Here the outside wall was finished and thick as a lance was long, well able to withstand any assault the Saxons might try to make. It could probably withstand even the stones of a catapult.

After the main gates, we passed through the outer court and took the next hill at the gallop. At the top, Lord Artos reined to his right, passed an unfinished inner wall, and rode into a large court that was separated from the active construction by a high wall. This somewhat muffled the bustle and the other sounds of building. We of the van followed him, but glancing back over my shoulder, I saw the rest of the troop taking a different direction. Then I looked forward again and had to catch my breath at the magnificence of the several-storied building in front of us.

The *Comes* kneed Cornix up the wide shallow flight of stairs, the stallion's metal sandals clattering on the stone. Bending over in his saddle, Lord Artos called out to those within.

"Come, you all, and see how well we shall be mounted to drive Aelle and his sons from Britain!"

Men and women swarmed out of the edifice, startling Cornix so that he reared, pivoted on his hind legs, and came down so hard on his forehand that I was certain even as fine a rider as the *Comes* would be dislodged. But Lord Artos only laughed, placing such a firm hand on Cornix's neck that the animal came to a full and complete halt, snorting but obedient.

They gray I was on suddenly quieted, and at the same time I felt a pull on the reins. Looking down, I saw a lad in livery with his hand on the bridle. I was about to protest when those Lord Artos had summoned came down the stairs to examine the Libyans more closely.

Rhodri had trained the horses well, for although they rolled their eyes, they remained four square at the halt—almost, I thought, as if they knew they were on display.

"These have been covering all those mares you assembled, Artos?" asked a man—one of the Companions, to judge by his bearing. He ran a knowing hand down Victor's near foreleg. "And is this what made all that clanging?" he cried, fingering the rim of the iron sandal.

"Ah, so Canyd has finally succeeded with the hoof sandal?" And now the *Comes* glanced at me to verify that.

I nodded. "They are all shod, Lord Artos, to protect their hooves . . ."

" 'No hoof, no horse.' " Lord Artos roared with laughter, slapping his leg in high good humor. "Eh, there, Galwyn?"

I laughed, too, sitting that much straighter because he had singled me out as conversant with his jest.

"Horse sandals?" The phrase was bandied back and forth among the men who each came to inspect the device.

"Now, Artos"—and the first Companion came up to him, frowning—"is all this wise? Is it not one extra problem when facing battle?"

"Ah, Cei, Galwyn here can answer you on that score—can you not?"

I gulped. Cei's blue eyes were very keen and I knew I had to answer him cleverly. "The sandals protect the feet of these big horses, who must bear more weight than even the largest of the ponies, my lord Cei."

"How are they fitted on? Nails? They'll work out, and then the sandal could shift and the horse be lamed . . ."

"The nails are clinched downward so they cannot work out. The sandal is fitted hot so as to conform to the hoof, for every hoof is different and every sandal is made to fit the hoof . . ."

"But who is to keep the sandal repaired? Even iron will abrade on stony roadways."

"Men are being trained to this work, my lord."

"And you are one of them, are you not, Galwyn?" Lord Artos said.

"I brought along extra sandals for each of the stallions, and nails. It is a simple matter . . ."

"Not if the nail goes into the quick of the hoof," objected Lord Cei, but I could see his interest was more curious than critical. He wanted to understand the whole procedure.

"There is a sufficient wall of horn in the hoof, my lord, into which the nail can be sunk. Most smiths are accustomed to trimming hooves. They will know how carefully to go."

"I'd rather have you here to attend to the matter," Lord Artos said.

"Lord"—and now I began to stutter—"I am still in need of much training in the care of the hoof and its ailments. Canyd said—"

"Well, if he has had the training of you, I don't worry at all." Lord Artos dismissed my doubts with a wave of his hand.

"But, Lord Artos, I am not yet completely trained. I could not take on such a responsibility."

"Arlo—" and the *Comes* raised his voice, gesturing to a young man in livery to come to him—"go to Ilfor the smith and ask him to attend me. Tell him Canyd's finally made those horse sandals he's been threatening to provide. And where are the other sandals, Galwyn? In your packs? Fetch Galwyn's packs, too!"

By then, other Companions had gathered about us, inspecting Victor's sandals, exclaiming over their appearance and purpose. I was required to answer endless questions; and when the smith and my supplies arrived at the same moment, I had to pass around the spare sandals and the nails, plus all the equipment that I used to shape the hoof and nail the sandal on.

Ilfor the smith asked more searching questions than anyone and seemed skeptical of the whole idea, turning a sandal over and over in his big work-scarred hands.

At some point, the Libyans were taken off to be stabled and fed. One of the grooms looked vaguely familiar—the set of his head and the way he hunched slightly. Could it be—Iswy? I wondered. Then I scoffed at myself. This person was taller and bearded. I mustn't be looking for Iswy all over the kingdom. How could someone like Iswy be in Camelot?

Then I was escorted into the building, with little time to assess its wonders while I explained, yet again, about these remarkable horse sandals. I barely had time to eat the evening meal that seemed a feast to me.

When torches were lit and everyone replete with food and wine—though I drank naught but small beer—I was finally allowed a respite from the Companions' searching questions. Only then did I finally sit back and get my bearings.

We were seated in a chamber with a high-vaulted ceiling, at a large round table. This was a departure from the Roman style of dining, though still affording the guests the opportunity to face each other. This table dominated the upper third of the hall. The *Comes Britannorum* sat at the top of this round table, his chair larger and more ornately carved than the backless ones in which we of lesser rank were seated.

On the far side of the stone pillars that supported the roof were smaller offices, where the Companions assisted the *Comes Britannorum* in the management of his domain. Doors led off to other rooms, and a stairway circled up to the upper floors of the building and its annexes. The whole building was a fine place from which Lord Artos would rule his province and send forth his troops of black horses. I had never been in such a grand place, although my father's villa had been accounted a fine home.

I was so tired that I could not pay close attention to the conversations that went back and forth and around the table. I vaguely remember that the talk that evening, as every evening afterward, was inevitably centered on the *Comes's* plan to unite the neighboring tribes. His arguments had not changed a bit from the plans he had told us those evenings around our campfires on the road to and from Septimania. But his words were spoken with much more conviction: as if he had refined reason and argument after constant debate on the issues.

That evening they were discussing, as well, how to

involve the Catuvellavnii, whose lands lay closer to the Saxon menace. Representatives from that province were due to visit Lord Artos soon: one of the reasons he had wanted the Libyan horses here to display. But the discussions—though they were interesting to me in terms of how Lord Artos won his supporters—were well beyond my attention that night.

When I had finished my meal, I was shown to the guest cubicles, where I was accorded a bed to myself— a luxury I appreciated after six days on the road.

DESPITE MY FATIGUE and the weariness of the previous night's questionings, habit was strong and I was awake at dawn's light. Dressing quietly so as not to disturb the other sleepers, I found my way out of the castle and to the stables.

The early-morning routine was in full progress, most of the horses already watered and fed by their grooms, even my Spadix. He and Cornix were, of course, stabled together. I wondered who had decided that that was necessary, but I felt that Cornix, and Spadix, had undoubtedly made their wishes known. Someone had even combed the pony's thick mane, and Cornix's sleek coat gleamed with deep blue lights. As usual, Cornix whickered at the sight of me and Spadix added his comments in a shriller tone.

"You didn't need to come," said a lad whom I remembered as the one who had led *Comes* Artos's gray stallion. He erupted out of the next stall, a pitchfork in one hand. Dark-haired, gray-eyed, and wiry in build, the lad almost seemed to resent my appearance.

"Habit, I fear," I said with what I hoped was a rueful

smile. I was a guest in this place and had no rank at all. Perhaps I was offending the order of these stables by appearing unasked.

"You're the one who made the horse sandals," he added, more suspicious than ever.

"I'm *learning* how," I said with emphasis, and saw him relax his guard a trifle. Cornix pushed his nose at me for a caress and ducked his head so I could scratch his ears.

The boy's eyes widened. "He knows you."

"He should. He's been in my charge since Lord Artos bought him at Septimania."

"You went there with the *Comes?*" His surprise doubled and I could see a grudging respect in his manner, which I couldn't fail to appreciate. I smiled back, warming to the lad, seeing in him traces of what I had been like a scant year before.

"I was, and I sailed back with him, Cornix, and my pony Spadix, here." I could be proud of that adventure.

He gawped, his chin dropping as he was finally impressed by my *bona fides*. I slapped Cornix familiarly on his strong thick neck.

"I rode Cornix here—until Lord Artos claimed him on the road."

"So that's why you were up on Ravus," he said.

"The gray?"

He nodded.

"Yes, we changed mounts. That's a fine beast! Lovely gaits and a beautiful mouth. Do you have charge of him as well?"

He was ready to be civil now. "I'm Eoain Albigensis,"

he said, giving his formal name, and we clasped each other's forearms in the fashion of friends. "Are *all* the Libyans as grandly big as these?"

"Only the best would do Lord Artos," I said, trying to sound more matter-of-fact than pompous. "And the mares are every bit as fine as the stallions. You should see this year's foals. Fifteen were born in February, and every one sturdy. Cornix, here"—and the animal whuffled, pricking his ears forward at the sound of his name—"did his duty by every mare he covered. All of the fifty proven in foal."

"Fifty?" Eoain's eyes bulged at such a prodigious number.

"Well, we have to mount all the Companions on animals as good as these, don't we?"

He nodded his head, eyes still wide. "And you've to make sandals for 'em all?"

I laughed. "I won't be the only one, I assure you."

I was just about to ask him if there was a Cornovian named Iswy working in the stables when the slender young lad Lord Artos had called Arlo appeared in the stableyard, breathless from the speed of his run.

"Eoain, Lord Artos and his Companions will ride out on the Libyans to hunt after mass." Then he noticed me. "You're Galwyn?" he asked, not quite disrespectful, more uncertain. When I nodded, he added, "Because Lord Artos wishes you to wait upon Ilfor the smith after mass. About those horse sandals." Then he pivoted on one heel and raced back the way he had come. Arlo, it seemed, rarely walked anywhere.

"You have a chapel here?" I asked Eoain.

What with my broken arm and then all the work on

the sandals with Alun and Canyd, I had not had the opportunity to get to mass at Deva as I had resolved to in the New Year. At the farm, one of the priests—usually an old one who better understood the peculiar attitude toward religion where most of the inhabitants were inclined toward a familiar semipaganism—made the trip to baptize infants or preside at a burial when needed. But they did not hold services. I was, therefore, almost hungry to attend a proper mass in a real church.

"Of course," Eoain said, obviously surprised that I would ask. He pointed to a high slate roof that could be seen from the stableyard, at the other side of the great hall. "Mass will be said shortly, so you'd better hurry."

"But if I'm to go to Master Ilfor—"

"You'd best go to mass first, Galwyn," he said firmly. "Master Glebus does and I will. Lord Artos and his Companions do."

My indecision lasted no longer than his final sentence. So that morning, and every morning thereafter of my stay at Camelot, I stood with the throng of worshipers in a church that was as perfect for Camelot as everything else about Lord Artos's castle. The church faced east and west, with high slit windows letting in a morning light that bathed the whitened walls in glorious shades of lemon yellow and pure white.

It was a joy to me to chant the responses, letting my heart savor the beautiful words. For one brief instant as the mass started, I thought I had forgotten the prayers, but then my tongue worked before my mind and the words came from the heart that had not forgotten them. If others merely mouthed the Latin, having learned the British tongue as their first language, I raised my voice—just slightly—to speak the purer sounds that had been drilled into me. The strength of my voice caused Eoain to give me a wondering look, and he sighed as if in relief.

By the Benedictus, I experienced a profound renewal of spirit, for I had not been aware of how much I had needed the benediction of the mass. I vowed to renew my religious duties with vigor, even if, at Deva, I would have to rise before dawn to attend. At least once a month. I promised that to God, if he would further Lord Artos's cause.

WHEN MASS WAS OVER, the lords made their exit first, passing through the lesser worshipers. Lord Artos cast his eyes to left and right as he proceeded, and he caught sight of me, giving his head a slow nod as if pleased to see me in the congregation. I was all the more glad that I had come this first morning in Camelot. I had been a sorry Christian these past few years and was joyous to have my faith also renewed today: another benefit of my service to Lord Artos.

When we, too, finally processed out of that lovely church into the sunlit morning, it was still early enough. Mass evidently did not intrude on the business of the day.

Eoain pointed out to me the way to Ilfor's forge. I detoured first to my cubicle and collected my packs of horse sandals and tools. Pausing briefly in the kitchen, I took a handful of the cold meats and bread set out on the trestle tables, and these I munched as I strode to my appointment. The unfinished outer court was already crowded with people and stacks and piles of the supplies which had been among the loads brought in the day before. Workmen were struggling up ladders with tiles; nets of rock were being hoisted to the masons awaiting them on the heights, and carpenters banged merrily away at various other projects.

Alun's forge at Deva had been generous in size but Camelot's was immense: sprawling from one vast cavern to another across the one completed wall of the castle. I don't know how many smiths there were working metal at their anvils, but obviously Ilfor was an important person to have charge of so many.

Master Ilfor, however, broke off the orders he was giving two underlings and whirled on me as if I had lost an entire day's work. I had not seen him at mass and somehow did not think I ever would. Later, I would learn that religious tolerance was a part of Lord Artos's way of dealing with diverse people and attitudes.

"I want to see these sandals of Canyd's," he said, scowling. He had not seemed so critical the night before. But then, Lord Artos had been present. Now I was in the smith's own domain, and considerably inferior to him in rank. When I went to remove some sets from my packs, he shook his thick hand. "No, not ones you brought. Show me how *you* make them."

"I made," and I stressed that word slightly because Ilfor had the look of a bully and I would no longer let myself be a victim, "all those." I was also feeling extremely charitable after the cleansing effect of hearing mass.

"Show me," he repeated, and he gestured peremptorily

at a handily empty anvil at the nearby fire. Then he folded his heavily muscled arms across his chest, obviously skeptical.

I shrugged; diffidence is a good defense against men of his temperament. I knew, as I withdrew my leather apron from my pack and laid out my tools on the anvil's pedestal, that I did not look as much a smith as he. I had neither his bulk nor his sinew. Nor could I fold metal for a sword and hammer the blade into shape, nor make arrows and lanceheads or shields and breastplates as he could. But horse sandals I could fashion quickly, deftly, and have them fit the horse that needed to be shod.

"Where is the horse?"

"Horse?" he asked, widening his eyes. "Why would you need a horse?"

"To fit the sandal to, of course," I replied, undaunted.

"Make the sandal!"

There was no evasion from that command. I shrugged and, walking to where his store of iron was kept, selected a length that would be suitable for a pony sandal. No, not a pony! I realized I had the gray stallion in mind. Why not sandals for Ravus? Lord Artos rode him often.

I had acquired the habit of checking the feet of any horse I rode, assessing how wide, or narrow, a sandal would be to fit the beast. I had done so the day before with Ravus. That trick of observation stood me in good stead now.

I nodded to the bellows boy to stoke up the fire, and I thrust the metal into its reddening coals. I turned it until the center was bright orange and, grabbing it with my tongs, began with my hammer to curve a sandal out of the shapeless length.

There is a joy in working metal, in watching it take the shape you have in your mind—as if you have been able to translate form from mind to matter. I heated and bent the metal several times to obtain the appropriate semicircle. I then heated and flattened it within that form to match the gray's feet. I heated it again to make the nail holes, hammering the iron spike through the pliant metal. Then I thrust it into the water butt and began the second sandal.

All the while Ilfor watched with narrowed and suspicious eyes. But for the fact that I had been accustomed to the constant appraisal of both Alun and Canyd, the doubt and challenge in his face and stance would have made me nervous. Of course, once engrossed in the making of the sandals, I actually forgot him in the rhythm of the work.

When I had finished the set, I looked up at him questioningly. He reached in among the sandals I had brought with me and took out a pair, tied by a thong. These he compared to the ones I had just finished, and snorted.

"Much too small if these are for those Libyan blacks," he said almost contemptuously.

"They have all the sandals they'll need for the year," I said calmly. "I made this set for that gray desert stallion Lord Artos rode yesterday."

"You did?" And his brows went up. At his imperious gesture, the bellows lad came quickly to his side and was told to go ask Master Glebus at the stableyard to send up the gray.

Once again he folded his arms across his chest and waited with the patience of someone who is confident of success in humbling a braggart. And something more. It was as if he knew something about me: something to my discredit. He was waiting to see if I could do what I had so glibly described to the Companions.

I thought suddenly about the young man I had seen last night who had seemed so familiar. Could it have been Iswy after all, putting a word in the smith's ear? I had grown taller; why not Iswy? I hadn't known his age but possibly he was old enough now to have grown a beard, too. But surely a man of Master Ilfor's standing would pay no attention to snide remarks by a groom.

Not to let Ilfor's regard or my own suspicions unnerve me, I took out my sack of horse sandal nails, wedged ones I had made myself to Alun's design. I put hammer and rasp where they would be easily to hand, and then I likewise waited, hands tucked into the ties of my leathern apron.

Master Glebus himself led the gray to us, the bellows lad trotting behind him. The boy's eyes were avid with anticipation of my downfall.

"Sa-sa-sa," I murmured in Canyd's way to the gray, for he didn't like being close to the fire. He twitched his delicate ears back and forth nervously at all the loud clangings and bangings. I stroked his neck and withers, working my hand down the near leg to the fetlock, which I then tugged up. He had a strong deep hoof that needed only a little trimming. But I had something to prove first. I picked a sandal out of the water butt and laid it on the hoof.

I admit to a smile of triumph when I heard a quick

gasp of surprise from the lad. I did not look at Ilfor, but Master Glebus certainly noted the excellent fit.

"However did you do that, lad?" he asked. "Why, they fit as if they were made for him."

"They were," I said, letting the hoof down as I confronted Master Ilfor.

He scowled and gestured for me to fit the other front hoof. I changed sides and showed that the second sandal was as close a match to the horse's hoof as ever the first had been.

Ilfor gave one grunt.

"Shall I put the sandals on?" I asked Master Glebus, for he had charge of the horses and it was wise to get his permission.

"Yes, I should like to see how it is done," he said without so much as a glance in the smith's direction. He knew, without being told, what had occurred here in the smithy. His attitude toward me was so positive I began to think that I really hadn't seen Iswy last night. So, with some relief, I threw the first sandal back into the fire to heat, for nailing it on hot made for the best fit.

The gray was not as easy to work on as the Libyans, who had grown to trust me. In fact, he was completely rebellious, despite my best efforts at soothing him. It looked for a while as if he was more likely to leave here sandalless, which made nothing of my gesture in making so perfect a rim for his feet.

But Master Glebus was an old hand at dealing with fractious horses. He wound a stout rope about the end of the gray's nose and twisted it hard. The twitching gave Ravus something to think of other than his feet.

I worked as swiftly as I could with the hot sandals, placing each nail and measuring how it would enter the hoof at the correct angle so as not to prick the tenderer part of the foot. I clinched the nails, pinched off all but enough of the metal to bend down in the clinching, and hammered the ends down into the outside of the hoof. With a final application of the rasp to the nail end, I smoothed the hoof so that no one's hands would be snagged on a jagged metal edge.

Released from the nose twitch, the gray snorted in relief, shaking his head, until he became aware of the extra weight on his hooves. The sandals sent sparks flying from the cobbles and clanged with the energy of his movements, but he could not dislodge them. Gradually he walked into the feel of them.

"Any more you'd like shod, Master?" I asked, more to the horsemaster than to the smith.

Ilfor grunted again. Then suddenly, like the sun appearing on a gray day, a smile appeared on his soot-grimed face, showing large white teeth crooked in a full mouth. He also extended his large hand.

"You *do* know what you're about in a forge, lad, for all there's little brawn to you," he said. "Neat, tidy, quick." He gave his head a decisive nod, as if he had been reserving his opinion all the while I worked. He took my hand, pumping it and squeezing my fingers in his powerful ones: obviously a man who did not know his own strength.

I caught the sympathetic expression on Master Glebus's face, as if he well knew what pressure my hand was experiencing, and so I endured the clasp without wincing. But Master Ilfor's wording—that suggested something had been said to him about me and he had been weighing judgment. Perhaps Eoain could tell me. Now I felt it wiser to reinforce the goodwill where I had it.

"I only do sandals, Master Ilfor, but those I do well," I said with the same simple authority with which Canyd would speak, "serving the *Comes Britannorum* to my utmost. Just as you do."

Master Ilfor gave another of his grunts but his manner suggested that I had made the right reference: that we both served Lord Artos in our different ways.

"I've a gelding," Master Glebus said, raising one finger tentatively, "badly crippled with seedy toe. Would those iron rims . . ."

"Just what the sandals are for, Master Glebus," I replied, smiling my willingness.

I SPENT THE ENTIRE DAY in the forge, after first formally requesting permission from Forgemaster Ilfor to use his facilities. I made sandals for cracked, damaged hooves so that the ponies might stride out again pain free. Master Ilfor having made a tactful mention of how much iron he needed to continue his own work, I merely trimmed hooves that were not in such immediate need of sandals.

By the end of the week, I had worked my way through all the horses and ponies connected with Camelot, for many that were not needed on a daily basis were pastured nearby. I even did some of the farm animals that were hauling the carts up the road to the castle. They needed such rims as protection, perhaps more than the riding horses. And I willingly trimmed the feet of oxen, for they had problems as well, treating such puncture wounds and bruises as I discovered.

I was aware that, while I worked, one or another of the other blacksmiths turned up to watch the sandal making and were especially attentive during the fitting. Such scrutiny amused me, for I realized that Ilfor was making sure all his men would know how to fit the sandals. But there was more to it than watching someone else work. Nor would I be here much longer, for I would soon be returning to the farm at Deva.

Ilfor's men, no matter how carefully they watched, needed special training. Lord Artos might have mentioned that he wanted me to stay on, to continue to practice my skill, but I knew how much more I had to learn. When I felt myself to be truly competent, *then* I would return here.

However, I was very much aware that we all served Lord Artos. Therefore, on the third morning, I approached Master Ilfor and suggested that he might like to have one or two of his smiths work along with me in making and fitting the sandals.

Ilfor at first expressed surprise at my suggestion, as if his men had only been "watching," not memorizing the steps. Then he smiled, rubbing one large ear with two fingers as he realized that I had realized what he was about.

"We both serve Lord Artos," I reminded him, allowing him that much leeway. "We are still learning how best to protect the feet. No foot, no horse!"

He nodded soberly at the saying and immediately delegated four of his apprentices to my tutoring. None of them were at all skeptical about the merits of the sandals, having seen once-lame horses walk, sound, out of the smithy with the fitted sandals.

By chance I heard from Master Glebus that a horse had been put down for a broken leg. So I begged to prepare one hoof so that the students would learn, as I had, from a close examination of a horse foot. A gory task, but essential if I was to be a proper tutor.

I TALKED MORE FOR the next three days than I had ever talked in my life. I sent the apprentices out to find unshod horses to practice on. Although I tried to avoid such a problem, it turned out that the one nail-bind that occurred—from a nail sunk too close to the tender part of the foot—made my four students more conscious of the damage inattention to detail could wreak.

I talked, I explained, I demonstrated. The metal fabrication was never a problem with men already skilled at forge work, nor was making the special tools required to do the actual fitting. But metal is dead; a horse is living. They had to learn how to cope with the horse, the hoof, the hammer, and the nail. Gradually, though, I could see confidence building as they acquired a certain knack in the doing.

Since I was free to move about Camelot, I did so, looking for another glimpse of the man I thought was Iswy. I had none, but then he could have been there and gone: Camelot had constant visitors, each with attendants.

"Don't know anyone by that name," Eoain told me when I got a chance to ask him. "Not among the stable lads."

"Anyone new here—"

Eoain's laugh interrupted me. "New? With all the comings and goings right now? If you're worried about Cornix and your pony, don't. Master Glebus is real careful about who he lets work *our* horses," he added, pushing out his chest pridefully.

I certainly hadn't seen anyone remotely resembling Iswy since that first glimpse.

"Any Cornovians?" I asked.

Eoain shrugged. "I don't ask such questions." Then he had a thought. "Plenty of people coming in to work out there . . ." And he waved at the outer courtyard.

"Iswy would work with horses." Unless of course, I added to myself, Bericus had seen to it that no one hired him to care for animals ever again.

Eoain shook his head. "We've had half a dozen lads coming in and out with our guests' horses over the past few days. If he was here, he's gone now."

That was all the reassurance I was likely to find, and really I had far too much else to do to fret over a man who was leagues away from Camelot now—even if he had been here one night.

MY LAST TWO MORNINGS at Camelot I spent teaching the apprentices what I had learned from Canyd of remedies for common hoof ailments like seedy toe, sand cracks, hoof rot, and the puncture wounds that were so prevalent. They listened, but I think that most of them thought that such knowledge was redundant: They would do whatever Master Glebus or the horse's owner required them to do.

That was a smith's view of metalworking but not

mine. Nor Canyd's. However, the apprentices learned much and were no longer as skeptical of my craft. That, in itself, was a huge step forward.

On my first free afternoon I went to watch Lord Artos and the Companions working the big Libyans, and that was a magical time. The warhorses seemed to enjoy the maneuvers they were asked to perform. What a splendid sight for the watcher! The stallions entered wholeheartedly into the exercise as they charged down the field at imaginary targets. I could guess what the feelings of an enemy might be, faced with those great black steeds, nostrils flaring, teeth bared. Rhodri would be gruffly pleased with my detailed account of the display.

I spent my evenings listening to the Companions, and listening to the visitors who were mostly trying to avoid joining Lord Artos's combined army. I remembered what Lord Artos had said that one night when we were around the campfire: that God had given man free will, and it was up to men to make the proper choices in their lives, choices that would lead them to places in heaven. I had not had much time for philosophy on board the *Corellia*, during the long months in my uncle's service. Not even at the farm in Deva. But in Camelot I gave much thought to the world and my place in it. Would that I could join the force that Lord Artos was now training! And who would train me as a swordsman? Maybe as a slingsman, for Yayin was handy with that Cornish weapon. But slingsmen were foot soldiers, and I wanted to ride a Libyan stallion into battle! *Ah well*, I thought philosophically, *at least I have been to Camelot!*

Camelot was such an amazing place, truly every bit as marvelous as I'd been told. I knew myself to be fortunate indeed. So I did not protest when one of the stewards called me from the forge to meet with the *Comes* the day before I was to leave.

HE WAS IN THE ROOM that he used as office, seated at a long sturdy table cluttered by scrolls, bits of leather, two sheathed knives, and scraps of parchment covered with notes in a bold script. There were shelves for the scrolls; lances standing propped against one corner; and Lord Artos's sword, Caliburn, and its scabbard neatly racked up on the wall nearest the door, ready to hand should he be called in an emergency.

He had before him the scroll I had brought from the farm, enumerating the mares known to be in foal, and to which stallions.

"Ah, Galwyn, now that you've taught Master Ilfor's men what they need to know"—and he grinned at me, aware as always of all that went on in his castle—"we can continue the good work started by yourself . . ."

"More by Masters Alun and Canyd than me, Lord Artos," I said hastily.

"I like a modest man, Galwyn." I straightened my shoulders, for he called me *man* now, not *lad*. "But I also give credit where it's due. It is due you, Galwyn Varianus." And he extended me a pouch that I could hear clinking as he hefted it.

"I'm only glad to have been of service, *Comes*," I said, keeping my hands behind my back.

With a swoop, he pulled my right arm forward and firmly placed the pouch in my resistant hand.

"And worthy of some reward for months of honest service and dangerous work." He closed my fingers around the leather bag. "I shall not say farewell, Galwyn"—and his eyes twinkled at me—"for undoubtedly we shall need your special skills . . . once you consider yourself well-enough trained." His smile was both amused and understanding. "So now I shall merely wish you a safe journey back to Deva. Especially if you will act as messenger with these." And he passed over a half-dozen tightly wound scrolls, with a long strip of parchment tucked under the thong that bound them together. "The names of the recipients are written on each, and directions to each one on that strip. Your road to Deva takes you close to all. You'll get a decent meal or a night's shelter on your way as my messenger."

"Of course, Lord Artos—" And then I stuttered to a full stop. I didn't know how to continue because, of course, the messages should be delivered quickly and Spadix must stay with Cornix. I could only go so fast on foot, for I was not a runner that some are. I did hope to find a farm cart or two or even a wagon train along the way to give my feet a rest.

Then he burst out laughing. He had the most infectious laugh, so I had to grin back at him. "I've taken Spadix from you, haven't I, for that sentimental barbarian of a Libyan. Well, as my messenger, you must naturally have a suitable mount. He awaits you. I shall look forward to our next meeting, Galwyn Varianus. A hundred more like you at my back, and no Saxon army could withstand us!"

Thus, chest swelled with pride, I left his presence and hurried out to the courtyard. I would miss Spadix, though not as much as I might once have done; I'd grown too tall to be very comfortable riding him. But he would always have a special place in my heart. After all, he'd carried me bravely into a completely new life.

I did not, however, anticipate the mount awaiting me—the African gray! And wearing, under the saddle, a pad with Lord Artos's distinctive device of the bear. Tied to the saddle was a cloak, also in the colors of the man I served, and leathern pouches to protect the scrolls from weather and dust. All would know me for a messenger of the *Comes Britannorum* and respect me as such.

Master Glebus himself was there, smiling with great pleasure at my astonishment.

"Surely there's some mistake, Master Glebus!" I exclaimed. "He's much too—"

"Nonsense, lad, with the new Libyan to amuse the *Comes*, he is not likely to ride this fellow as much as Ravus needs. He's also to do his bit with the mares, for we can always use more messenger horses with his turn of hoof and endurance. He's a good do-er and will keep condition if he only smells oats now and then. Further"—and now Glebus leaned into me with a hand cupping his mouth—"Lord Artos in full regalia is too heavy for his back. The Libyan suits him better in that regard: an animal well up to weight." He straightened up, winking. "You're a messenger right now, too, so the gray's speed is to your advantage. You know your first destination?"

I glanced down at the slip—it was nearly transparent with all the messages that had been inscribed and then scraped off its surface. My first stop would be outside Aqua Sulis at an armorer's, one Sextus Tertonius's, a destination which I could make easily on this fine horse by evening—if I started immediately.

"You'll be fed and bedded on the way, lad. No fear of that as the *Comes*'s messenger."

I took the reins from Master Glebus's hand and vaulted to the stallion's back. He pranced in place under me until I soothed him with my voice and a hand on the arching crest of his neck.

"Good speed, lad," the horsemaster said, stepping back. I pressed my knees into the trembling sides of my mount and began my journey back to the farm.

AS SOON AS WE HAD MANAGED to descend from the heights of Camelot, I let the fidgeting Ravus have his head and he went forward at a gallop, his hooves ringing against the paving stones. He was fresh and I honestly did want to test his gaits. He was so agile that we had no difficulty in weaving around those on their way to Camelot. I even heard a few cheers.

I thought I heard an echo of a curse, and looking over my shoulder for fear I had inadvertently caused trouble, I did see another mounted rider some distance behind me. His animal was not as clever footed as mine, and the rider had run right into a team of oxen dragging a sled full of granite.

I stroked Ravus's neck, well pleased with his

dexterity, and let him continue his gallop. He had sense enough himself to drop down to a canter, an easy gait for a rider to relax into.

I reached my first destination, the armorer's, where Sextus Tertonius himself greeted me, emerging from the smoky interior of his forge, where half a dozen men were busy at anvil and hearth. He called one lad to take my horse away to be unsaddled and refreshed.

"For you will surely need to rinse the travel dust from your throat, Galwyn," Sextus said, and then wrenched his head around at the sound of Ravus's shod feet on the bricks of his yard. "Whatever is the matter with him?"

I grinned, signaling the lad to stop. "Sandals to protect his feet from prods and bad surfaces."

So, although Ravus was unsaddled, he had to stand about and let me pick up his feet one by one to show Sextus his iron rims.

Tertonius shook his head, drawing his mouth up into a pucker. "Don't see the need of such things, lad. Choose a horse with a good strong upstanding hoof and you'll have no problems, whatever you ride him over. But that Artos"—and he shook his head again—"he's got a lot of fancy notions in that head of his, as he'd be better without."

Sextus Tertonius was the first smith who did not see the benefit of the horse sandals. But he was by no means the last. I only hoped that he would give Lord Artos's message a more positive response than he'd given the sandals.

I had a meal while Ravus was washed down,

groomed, fed, and readied for me to ride off to my next stop.

I WAS ENCOURAGED TO STAY under cover that night at my third stop, a villa outside Corinium; indeed, the weather had worsened. But my night's rest was broken by the dogs barking sporadically all night and by the thunder and lightning of a fierce storm. While I didn't rise, my hosts did, investigating each new outbreak of alarm. In the morning I asked what had aroused them.

"Chicken thieves," my host said, shrugging. "We've foxes as well as ferrets hereabouts and they do go for the chickens."

Ravus was as fresh as if he hadn't done leagues the day before, and I had to let him gallop the fidgets out until he would settle once more to his easy but distance-eating canter.

In Corinium, too, I took a good-natured dismissal of the horse sandals from the recipient of Artos's message.

"And what happens if a nail works loose? You've to walk the horse then, haven't you, to whomever can fix it?"

"I know enough to do that," I replied evenly. I had become so used to a positive attitude toward the sandals that such skepticism made me reticent.

"And weigh yourself down more with hammer and nails, I'll warrant," was the reply.

So I handed over the message, courteously refused any hospitality, and rode on to Glevum. There I delivered the last of my messages, but Prince Geneir insisted that I could take time now to rest my horse and myself before proceeding onward to Deva. I was glad enough, for Glevum is a considerable town and I had a few odd coins to spend, given me by the satisfied owners of horses I had shod.

I wandered around the market and bought a set of large wooden spoons for Daphne, who was forever breaking hers, generally on the scullery maids' hands for being sloppy or slow. I bargained hard for a cloak fastener for Canyd and bought a hot meat pie from a vendor. Then I sat on the wall at the edge of the marketplace to watch the folk coming and going. No one so grand as I had seen at Camelot, but it was so rare for me to have a day in which to please myself that I enjoyed the leisure for its own sake.

When I got back to the prince's house, there was a huge commotion in the stableyard; Prince Geneir himself was shouting orders. As soon as he saw me, he waved me urgently to him.

"Someone tried to steal that gray of yours, Galwyn."

A spurt of fear was quickly masked by the outrage I felt.

"Was the thief caught?"

Geneir gave an exasperated growl, his fingers rattling the hilt of the sword at his waist. "Slippery as an eel, he was, the moment my hostler remembered that Lord Artos's messengers travel alone. That's what the stable lad was told, that you were ready to leave. But the rascal didn't even know which bridle to use, and that made the boy suspicious, so he asked Gren. When Gren arrived to question him"—and now Geneir was as outraged as I—"he vaults to the gray's back and tries to ride him out of my yard, bareback and bridle-less. But my guards were alert and the gate was shut before he could leave. Gren said he was off the horse, up and over that wall there." And he pointed to the end of the stableyard where stood a high, vine-covered wall. "I've sent guards after him. He'll not get far."

If the would-be horse thief was Iswy, I doubted that—for the Cornovian was as clever as he was sly. We'd not been able to catch him at Deva for all the watching we'd done.

"What did the man look like? Did anyone see his face?"

Geneir beckoned his hostler, who was still red faced and puffing with indignation over the affair. "Did you get a good look at his face?"

"Aye, and a nasty look he had; raging, he was, at being thwarted."

"Was he bearded?" I asked.

The hostler nodded. "Raggedy-like. Tall as yourself, but skinny. Used to horses, though, the way he vaulted up, bareback and all."

"D'you know him, Galwyn?" asked Geneir.

Grimly I nodded, unable to speak for the fury that almost consumed me. First Spadix and Cornix, then Splendora, and now Ravus. So Iswy *had* been at Camelot, and he had doubtless been the rider I had seen behind me on the road. Quite likely, he was also the intruder who had kept the dogs barking in his attempt to get at Ravus in the stable.

"It's appalling that a messenger of the *Comes* should be hindered or attacked for any reason." Then a thought occurred to Geneir. "A Saxon spy?"

"I doubt it," I said, and then hesitated. A man who would deliberately cause harm to the horses he was supposed to value might grasp at other opportunities to do harm to those he hated. I couldn't at all be sure that he did not include Lord Artos in the category, but in my estimation Iswy was evil enough to turn treacherous, too. "No, I doubt he would have the opportunity, but he believes himself ill used in the service of Lord Artos," I said.

Geneir was clearly waiting for more of an explanation.

"He tried to injure one of the new Libyan stallions on our way to Deva and was sent off without a character. I believe he was guilty of other attempts to harm the Libyans."

"Ah, a vindictive type, is he?" Geneir touched his temple, nodding with complete understanding. "Never fear, Galwyn. We'll find him, and he won't bother you anymore."

"While your guards are after him, I should be on my way," I said with true regret and some honesty. "I *am* in Lord Artos's service, and there is another stop I should make to see if there are messages to be carried to Deva." Not true, but Prince Geneir accepted it.

I would have a good start on Iswy even if the Glevum guards did not catch him. And I'd travel by less well used roads so that no one would see me passing.

That is how I made it safely—and speedily—back to the farm at Deva.

I told Teldys of the incidents, and any time the dogs barked at night or the geese honked, someone went out to investigate.

More than a week later, Prince Geneir sent a regretful message that, despite the most diligent of searches, the culprit had not been caught. However, he had been traveling west and south when last sighted. When next Bericus came, unscathed from his latest skirmish with the Irish raiders, I reported Iswy's activities to him as well.

"I don't see Iswy as a spy either," Bericus said, "but I shall certainly warn Prince Cador and Artos to keep an eye out for him."

Part Five

GLEIN

AFTER A FEW MONTHS of constantly being on guard with no incidents or unexplained alarms, we gradually began to relax. While it was certainly an unchristian attitude, I did hope Iswy's sins had caught up with him somehow, somewhere else. At any rate, I became more engrossed in my training with Canyd and Alun, and in the nurture of the Libyan mares and foals.

I don't know where the time went to over the next few years, but months sped past, season sliding into season—from winter to spring, summer to autumn—and then the cycle of tasks to be accomplished began again.

I studied continually under Canyd, milking him of every scrap of information, determined to transfer his knowledge to my head. Who could know what obscure detail might be of a certain use to Lord Artos? I acquired three new apprentices and found that teaching was the most admirable way to remember, and refine, my own understandings. I fancied myself a good teacher, for my scholars seemed to understand my explanations *and* my cautions. Particularly about the position of the nails so as not to inadvertently puncture the thin wall of the protective horn and wound the foot with nail bind.

Smiths from distant provinces came themselves or sent other capable smiths for instruction. The farm was so busy that Teldys once complained—though in a teasing manner—that the sandals caused more company than the Libyans. But all were made welcome in Lord Artos's name.

"I dunna know why you keep badgering me, lad," Canyd Bawn said once when I kept after him over a foal's malformed hoof, which we were trying to reshape with the use of a special sandal. "For I tell ye, ye know as much as I do now."

"I'll *never* know enough," I replied fiercely, keenly aware that what I did know would not save the foal or allow him to gambol with the others in the field.

"Ay, then you've learned the most important lesson in your life," Canyd replied, nodding his head. He patted me on the shoulder. "A good man is what you are, Galwyn."

I only half listened to praise from such an unlikely quarter, because I grieved so at this failure.

"*Sa-sa*, lad, look at what you have done," Canyd said, waving at the horses being schooled by Rhodri that day, all of them striding out sound and sure in their sandals.

Though I was busy enough at the forge, making sandals and teaching others how to, from time to time I was also called on to deliver messages. That these excursions also gave me a chance to demonstrate the horse sandals elsewhere made the trips doubly beneficial. Certainly the state of Ravus's hooves proved the merit of using the sandals.

Ravus and I made many journeys from Deva to Camelot. If I saw Lord Artos at all on those occasions—and I would try to—he would solemnly ask me if I felt I had learned enough yet to come to Camelot.

"I am at your service at all times, Lord Artos," I would reply.

"So you are, good Galwyn, so you are!" he would say, one hand gripping my shoulder with what I liked to think was appreciation.

Once I rode all the way to Londinium with an urgent message for Artos from the princes of the Atrebates and Cantiacii. They needed his reassurance that he and his Companions would help keep the Saxons from moving south into their lands. I was told to verbally repeat the written message. It was an honor for me to do so.

Many of these journeys were not made at the headlong pace that pushed both Ravus and me to our limits. Those more leisurely trips were when we traveled to acquaint someone new with horse sandals. Most frequently, however, I went to Prince Cador's principal residence, for his horses required constant attention and his smith would not take time out from weapons manufacture to forge sandals. He didn't consider them important.

Prince Cador was one of Lord Artos's staunchest supporters, and when he was not fighting off invaders, he traveled much on the *Comes*'s behalf, arguing with other local princes and tribal leaders to join the noble cause and drive the Saxons back to the sea. His horses always seemed to lose their rims at awkward moments, requiring the prince to stay wherever he was until I could reach him to repair the problems. I began to suspect this was a ploy when three times in a row, the sandal was merely loose and a nail only needed to be tapped hard to solve the problem. But then, some people are difficult to persuade, and the silver-tongued prince of the Dumnonium liked nothing better than to sway men's minds to his thinking. I kept my counsel, though I often saw Prince Cador's amused eyes on me, as if he knew what was in my thoughts.

It was time again for Britons to take charge of their own defenses. Artos, as *Comes Britannorum*, was the obvious *dux bellorum*, since he had attracted many of the best warriors to his company.

ONE ADDED ADVANTAGE of my trips to, and with, Prince Cador was that these journeys allowed me to take occasional detours to keep my promise to my sister, Lavinia. And show off to my mother that I was now Lord Artos's messenger: in a position of trust to one of the most important men in Britain.

"That's a fine horse you're riding these days," Odran said, admiring Ravus, the first time I rode the gray to Ide.

"So you're back again," my mother said disagreeably as she came to the door.

"Only briefly, Mother." I peered around into the house to see if Lavinia was near.

"See the grand horse Galwyn is riding now," Odran said, pointing to the saddlecloth and the bear insignia.

"That's the *Comes*'s device," he added, obviously impressed.

"I ride as his messenger," I said proudly. Even Mother's usual disapproval could not dim the honor of that.

"So what can bring you here?" she demanded, waving dismissively to the small settlement by the old Roman fort.

But Lavinia, having heard my voice, came dashing around from the back of the house to throw her arms about my neck. "Galwyn! Galwyn! How grand to see you again! And Flora's had her baby, a strapping son, and Melwas so proud, too . . ."

"Can you stop long enough for a meal?" Odran hesitated when he heard my mother sniff. "Surely, wife, we can spare your only son a mug of beer."

". . . Oh, and such a grand horse as you're riding now! You have come up in the world, haven't you, Galwyn?" Lavinia said, lifting my spirits after my mother's cool reception. "There's a shady spot on the other side of the house where we can put your fine horse." She tried to wrest the reins from my hand.

"I'll do that," I said, smiling at her to show I appreciated her willingness.

"Then I'll get that beer for you." Odran made it plain to my mother that I was welcome in his eyes, if not in hers.

"I shall find Flora, then," Lavinia said. "She's dying to show you her son. They named him Gallus . . . after you . . . for your gold ring," she added in a whisper so Mother didn't hear. But her eyes were merry as well as grateful. "She'll be so glad to see you, Galwyn."

I loosened Ravus's girth and secured him to the tree, with a handful of grass to content him. Odran then ushered me into his house.

"Why did you have to take up with that warmongering Artos?" my mother asked, letting Odran pour mugs of the beer as she seated herself on the fireside stool.

"All Britain will one day be glad of the *Comes Britannorum*, Mother."

She gave a sniff.

"Then you think that the Saxons will invade—" Odran began.

"How would Galwyn know that, Odran?" she demanded. "He's only a messenger."

Odran raised his eyebrows and gave a little sigh. He was a good, patient man and my opinion was that my mother had been lucky indeed to find such a one.

I did not dispute her opinion of Lord Artos; there was no point. The sad fact was that, in my traveling, I had discovered many folk of the same mind. They firmly believed that the Saxons wouldn't come if no one irritated them. Fortunately, the majority were taking Artos seriously, especially as there were more rumors about Aelle and his sons increasing their soldiery. Sometimes these rumors were embroidered with lurid details about Saxon habits.

Flora arrived, breathless with carrying her sturdy child. She bore greetings and apologies from Melwas, who was slaughtering that day and could not come.

So I spent a very pleasant few hours with my sisters and Odran, playing with my nephew.

Before I left that afternoon, Flora had a quiet word

with me. Lavinia, now sixteen, was sincerely attracted to a young farmer and wished to marry him. But she had no dowry and his family needed what wealth a wife might bring.

"You were so good to give Melwas and me that gold ring, but we've used it all to improve the shop," she said, her face twisted with regret—but her unspoken question was all too clear.

I smiled back, for I was able to press into her hand four gold coins—of an old Roman minting—that I had in my pouch, received for messages I had delivered.

"Oh!" Flora exclaimed, turning them over, unable to believe I could have so much to give. "But Mother will—" And she half turned back to the house, for I was watering Ravus.

I took out a gold ring and showed it to her. "This I will give Mother," I said, and then I closed her fingers over the coins. "You see to Lavinia's dowry."

"Oh, Galwyn, you are so good to us. Uncle Gralior certainly would never have parted with this many coins." She put them carefully away.

"He's been to see you again?"

Flora made a face. "Too often. How you stood Uncle so long I shall never know! You're much better off as a messenger, even if Mother cannot see it."

I presented the ring to my mother on my departure, and she was so surprised that I had gold to give her that I thought I would never be able to take my leave.

"You will pass by again this way, won't you, my son?" she said, quite full of smiles now, and patting my chest with her hands.

I noticed that she tucked the ring into the bosom of

her dress as unobtrusively as possible. Odran might never profit from that generosity, but I could not find it in my heart to blame my mother. She had been accustomed to luxuries, and this austere life—for all she had a roof over her head and food on the table—must have been difficult for a proud woman to bear. I felt the better for sharing my good fortune with my blood kin.

SO I LEFT THE OLD FORT Ide with a cheerful heart and set Ravus into a canter. I thought to reach the wayside inn where I often stopped well before dark.

Following the winding road through the dense forests, I was not particularly surprised to come around a bend and find trees fallen across the track. I approached at a trot, for I wanted to see if there might be a way around the trunks; if not, how wide a jump it would be for Ravus.

We were about four strides away from the trees when suddenly men jumped out of the bushes, yelling and waving stout cudgels.

"Get him!" screamed a voice I had not heard in a long time but instantly recognized. *Iswy!*

"Bring down the horse! *Get him!*"

I clapped my heels to Ravus's side and the brave horse plunged forward and soared over the trunks, clearing them on the far side by a length or more.

"Go after him! Aim for the horse! Bring it down!"

Leaning down on Ravus's neck to make myself a smaller target, and urging the gray to his best speed, I did glance over my shoulder at my attackers. Three were clambering over the trees, their cudgels hindering their movements. Two, however, were whirling slingshots over their heads, and that was a real threat, for Cornovians were famous for their accuracy with sling and stone.

I kneed Ravus into a swerving course to make us a more difficult target. A stone glanced off his flank and he screamed, galloping even faster down the road. A second stone caught me on the right shoulder—the one I had twice dislocated—but by then its force had almost been spent. I gave no thought to my bruises, being far more worried about Ravus, though I didn't dare pull up until we were well down the road. We'd to cross a river farther on. I could stop there and still keep ahead of men on foot. But—what if they had mounts hidden in the woods?

I had traveled this way often enough, it was true, but how had Iswy known? I was almost sick with my fury over the ambush. Of course, this *was* the quickest route for me to take back to Deva from Isca. Was it mere chance that he'd seen me at Prince Cador's? He was, after all, a subject of Cador.

I forced myself to stop puzzling about Iswy and to think ahead about how I was to avoid pursuit. We should soon come to a stream. I could go either up or down it and come out on rocks farther up, so there would be less danger of being tracked.

Ravus was recovering from his fright by the time we reached the stream, and I could dismount, ignoring the chill of the water and the wetting of my good leather boots. I had to keep Ravus from drinking, hot as he was, and also stop him circling around me, so I could examine the bleeding wound.

It was shallow enough, for which I gave prayerful

thanks. I led him upstream to where moss grew on the rocks by the water. There I bathed the wound, pressing handfuls of cold water against it to stem the bleeding, because galloping had made it flow. The wound was also in an impossible place to bandage, but I took moss and pressed it so firmly against the cut that some would stick to the blood and seal it. I waited, listening for any sounds of pursuit, until I was certain the moss would hold. Then I led Ravus upstream until I judged we could safely enter the forest.

I found shelter that night in a glade where Ravus could graze, but I lit no fire and slept very poorly. The moss bandage stayed in place overnight and we continued on our way back to Deva by roads I rarely traveled.

I was going to insist that I be taught how to defend myself, and my horse.

TELDYS HAD ALREADY BEGUN to worry about me, knowing how swiftly I could make the journey. And when we arrived and I told the story of the ambush, everyone at the farm was concerned. When I asked Teldys if there was anyone on the farm with sword skills, he shook his head.

"None here, lad, nor even weapons to practice with. Come to think of it"—and he paused—"Yayin could doubtless teach you a few tricks with sling and dagger."

Fortunately, Ravus's wound showed no signs of infection, and that pleased Canyd.

"I only did as you would have done, Canyd," I said.

"And you see how right I am," the old man said smugly.

Still, I made a report to Bericus, relating the ambush and my suspicions about the assailants. We now took turns at night as sentries and always had someone in the stableyard to guard the Libyans.

"Iswy *was* seen at Isca," Bericus told me when he came on his next regular visit to the farm. His expression was grim. "There've been some raids on farmsteads near Ide. Would Iswy know that's where your mother lives?"

"He might. I've stopped there for brief visits before, and"—I sighed—"it's possible my family would have mentioned that I come there now and then on my way back from Prince Cador's. Could you not teach me how to use a sword?"

"I could, if there were time for such training. You are more valuable as a sandalmaker than a soldier or messenger," Bericus said. "You will travel no more alone." When he saw how disappointed I was, he gave me a reassuring buffet on my arm. "Don't be sad about losing mere messenger duties, Galwyn. You and Ravus will be traveling rather more than less, I think."

"Oh?"

He hooked his arm over the railing, for we were outside, by the field where Ravus was grazing.

"We've got to concentrate on mobilizing our army now . . . Yes," he said in answer to my gasp of surprise. "While I don't believe that Aelle is the devil incarnate, as some might"—and he chuckled at such superstitiousness—"there are definite indications that he's beginning to call in thanes, and certainly his armorers are busy. Not"—and now he grinned—"as if ours have been lazy these past few years, or haven't learned a few new skills, eh?"

"It's the horses that are going to win for us," I said staunchly.

"And every man who comes to Artos's banner wants one as his battle steed." Bericus turned and gazed out over the fields to where the latest crop of black and dark brown foals were cavorting.

Their antics reminded me of my first view of the Libyans charging down the practice field at Camelot. Just the memory made the hairs on the back of my neck stand up. Surely the sight of so many would daunt even the barbarian Saxons and send them scurrying back whence they had come!

"Well, we've mounted Gwalchmei, Geraint, Cei, Bedwyr, Medraut, Drustanus, Bwlch, and Cyfwlch; Prince Cador has three for battle and King Mark two . . ." I had no more fingers to count on. "All of the other Companions and half the chieftains and war leaders already pledged to support Lord Artos are now riding Libyan stallions."

"There'll be casualties," Bericus murmured, his expression sobering, and he sighed. "But"—and slapping both hands on the upper rail, he turned with renewed vigor to me—"we've more than fifty trained full-blooded Libyans right now. More than enough to cause the Saxons to think again about contesting the field with the *Comes Britannorum*."

"And Rhodri has ten more to be added to that number. Come, Bericus, he'll be in the training field," I said, and we made our way there.

TWO DAYS LATER, when I had put brand-new rims on those ten young horses, Firkin and I, in a large group of bowmen and slingshot mountain men under Manob's command, made our way to Camelot. I cast my eyes over every single foot soldier who made up that contingent; I almost wished that Iswy were among them so we could settle our enmity once and for all. I was now ready for him.

Following Teldys's advice after the ambush, I approached Yayin and asked him to teach me some defensive tricks with daggers. He could nail a rat to the wall from fifty paces and often did so, since rats were a constant menace in our oat store. Now I carried a well-honed bone-handled knife sheathed in my left boot. Yayin had also offered to teach me how to use a sling, but I hadn't the time to practice. A dagger would be a more useful weapon.

Manob set us as fast a pace as the foot soldiers could trot. And they seemed indefatigable, those wiry dark mountain men, still able to laugh and joke half the night around the campfire. I, on the other hand, had to check the sandals and hooves of the forty horses and was only too glad to roll up in my blankets at night.

AS WE MADE OUR WAY, we could feel a palpable tension in the villages and towns we passed through. Folks cheered the black horses as if they, in themselves, were the omen of victory over the Saxon hordes.

So I was actually in Camelot the day the exhausted messenger arrived, his horse so lathered that the beast looked gray rather than bay. The rider, of the Atrebatii, was covered with dust, sweat, and lather from his horse, and slid awkwardly from his saddle. He shrugged off assistance, demanding to be taken immediately to Lord Artos.

"They are moving," the man gasped. "Take me to the *Comes* . . ."

I went to the horse, who was all but foundered from the bruising pace at which he had been ridden.

Bericus hurried the messenger into the great hall, but the man paused at the top of the steps and looked back over his shoulder.

"Save him if you can!" he cried to me, his face contorted in anguish for the horse he had ridden so hard.

The bellows boy who helped me in Ilfor's forge was to hand, and between us we unsaddled the gasping animal and led him slowly into the stableyard. There we rubbed him down with twists of straw, and massaged his legs, and more carefully soothed his back; it had been rubbed raw in places by the rough saddle, which hadn't enough padding. We cooled him off enough to let him drink without endangering his recovery, and then we placed him in a stable, hock high with fresh straw, where he could rest.

I couldn't help noticing that his hooves were badly broken. He might yet recover but whether he would have any hoof left on the off-fore I didn't know, for it was cracked the worst of the four. *No hoof, no horse.*

I missed some of the early excitement, but by the time the bellows boy and I returned to the courtyard, the place was chaotic: men and lads rushing here and there; horses stamping and neighing, infected by their riders' excitement. I couldn't find Lord Artos in the mob, though I could hear his almost jubilant voice barking orders and occasionally bellowing great waves of laughter.

The waiting was over.

The scribes wrote so fast I wondered anyone could read their scrawls, but the written confirmation would scarcely be necessary. The bearers would have the meat of the news they bore—"Come with your men and your weapons. The Saxons are massing. The time is now!"

I found myself a space against the wall, wondering when I would be called to take a message, and to whom. But though I listened for my name, I did not hear it. I felt oddly isolated, as if everyone were going to war except me.

So I went back to the forge that Master Ilfor had allotted me, put on the leather apron I used when working, and prepared the fire for any horse that might need his sandals tightened. Then I went back into the great hall to find someone to report to. I couldn't find Master Glebus or Master Ilfor in the surging crowd.

Though I listened, I could not hear *where* the battle might be, nor *where* Lord Artos would be going. I caught city names like Corinium, Venonis, and Ratae; I heard discussions of the roads and their surfaces.

"So many can't forage . . ."

"The road to Durabrivae would be closer . . ."

"Do we wait or let the others catch us up?"

"Ha! Those mountain men can trot all day long without faltering . . ."

Torches were lit; men came and went.

I had learned a good deal of geography, and topography, during my messenger days, but some of the places named were unknown to me. Still, the excitement that pervaded the hall was contagious and made me, who seemed to have no part of it, very restless. Then I remembered the messenger's horse and chided myself for not checking on him sooner.

The stableyard was as busy as the castle, with hostlers leading saddled animals out or unsaddled ones in from the fields where extra mounts were kept. In the light of the torches—for the spring evening was closing into darkness—Master Glebus looked distraught, ordering this groom there, that horse saddled immediately, and where would he find more horses to send every which way? And it getting darker by the second.

I slipped in to check on the messenger's horse. He was lying down, nose to the straw, eyes closed. Softly I approached, not wishing to disturb his well-earned rest. I couldn't see well in the darkness, but when I gently touched the curved neck, it was dry and cool. And the animal was so deeply asleep he did not stir under my light touch. The water bucket outside the stall was empty; but the animal would be thirsty when he woke, and with all the excitement his needs might be forgotten. I also brought back a forkful of hay, for he would be hungry, too.

In the bustling kitchen, I found myself some bread and half a fowl to take back to my place in the forge, for I was certain that my services would be needed. There was much activity in and out of the great storeroom in which Master Ilfor kept the products of his hearths: men hurrying in empty-handed and coming out with sheaths of arrows and shields, or with lances and helmets, while others brought out the armor of their lords—helmets, shields, breastplates, arm and leg guards.

It was as I sat on a bench outside the busy kitchen, gnawing the last meat from the bone, that I saw him in the full light of the torches: Iswy, garbed in Cornovian colors, a sling and a bulging pouch of throwing stones hanging from his belt. Arrogantly he strode along. He was taller and he wore a scraggly beard, but his sharp face and close-set eyes had not changed. I almost choked on the meat and my left hand immediately went to the hilt of my knife.

Then I saw that not only did Iswy have his hand on the knife at his belt, but also he was heading toward the stableyard—where he certainly had no business, as a common foot soldier. I nearly choked again, instantly aware of why he had a hand on his knife and what he meant to do with that knife.

Losing his Libyan stallion would take the heart out of Lord Artos.

With all the confusion this night, and so many strangers coming and going, Iswy must have felt that he would be able to succeed in maiming, or killing, the stallion he had so wanted to ride. I darted after Iswy through the milling throng of serving men and attendants.

"Iswy! Stop! I want a word with you!" I called, but my shout was lost in the noise from the busy kitchen and the yard.

I had trouble weaving my way past cooks and soldiers carrying supplies to the waiting wagons. Outside,

I caught sight of Iswy, still striding across the courtyard toward the stable block. Again I called out.

"Stop that Cornovian!" This time my shout was masked by the creaking wheels of a heavily laden cart. I lost speed going around it and then tripped over packs that were waiting to be loaded on another cart.

Just then, someone caught my arm, and I had my dagger half out of its sheath before I realized he was finely dressed.

"You are Master Galwyn, the horse-sandal maker?" he asked.

"I am, but I—" I struggled to release myself from his grip.

"My steed"—and he pointed back over his shoulder—"needs your skills."

"Later, later."

"I beg your pardon." But he dropped my arm, dismayed and annoyed by my response.

"Take him to my forge. I must go—" I called over my shoulder at him as I renewed my pursuit of Iswy.

Dodging and weaving, I got to the entrance of the stableyard but could not see Iswy among those bustling about the yard.

"*Eoain! To Cornix!*" I shouted as I ran as fast as I could toward the corner stable, where Cornix and Spadix were kept.

I heard one short scream, unmistakably a horse's, cut off sharply.

The sound was enough to cause those in the yard to pause in their busy-ness.

"God in heaven!" I cried, and grabbed the nearest man. "Cornix is being attacked!"

"What?" An older groom caught me by the shoulder, swinging me around. "What say you? Oh, pardon, smith. What's the matter?"

Pulling him along with me, I pointed urgently toward the corner stable. "Cornix is being attacked . . ."

That startled him into action and he ran with me. But even as we raced to the corner stable, I could see the door swinging open.

"*Hurry!*" We would catch Iswy in the act, but what had happened to Cornix? My heart raced with fear. How could I tell Lord Artos that his battle steed had been spitefully maimed or killed?

"What's the matter?" Master Glebus appeared at my other side, and we all reached the stable at the same time.

I had to grab the door frame to keep upright. It was not Cornix who lay on his side in the straw but my faithful pony, Spadix, a dagger protruding between his eyes, in the thinnest part of a horse's skull. His dark eye was already filming with death.

"God above!" cried Master Glebus. "Who could have done such a wicked thing?"

"Iswy. He's Cornovian. I saw him come this way. No one else would want to kill Spadix."

I turned, looking out over the stableyard, trying to see any figure moving hastily out of the yard—but everyone was converging on us, not running away. "He can't have got far."

Master Glebus acted immediately, shouting for someone to run to the guards and close the gates. "The villain must be apprehended. I cannot have people slaughtering the animals in my care. What does he look like, Galwyn?"

"Wearing Cornovian, a head shorter than I, scraggly beard, slingsman," I said, now boxed into the corner by the press of men coming to see what had happened.

Maybe he'd be stopped at the gate. But there were still so many places in this section of Camelot in which a crafty man like Iswy could secrete himself. Oh, why had that lord stopped me? Why had no one been guarding Cornix?

I knelt beside my faithful old pony and closed his eyes. Then I yanked the knife from his skull and showed the hilt to Master Glebus.

"Aye, Cornovian design," he agreed. Then he put a consoling hand on my shoulder. "I'm sorry about this pony."

"Where *was* Cornix?"

"Lord Artos called for him not long ago, to greet some prince or other and show him off," Glebus said. "A lucky happenstance." When I sighed, he added quickly, "Unlucky for little Spadix. Cornix will grieve for him, too, I shouldn't wonder."

Eoain now pushed through and gasped to see Spadix dead in the hay. Tears sprang to his eyes as he dropped to his knees and began to stroke the pony's neck.

"I should have been here. I should have been guarding him, too. Who did such a vile thing?"

"Iswy, a Cornovian who held a grudge against him, and Cornix, and me."

"Oh!" Eoain looked up at me, tears flowing down his cheeks. He sniffed. "There's a princeling looking for you to put sandals on his horse and he's got Bericus with him. They're both very annoyed."

"Let them be!" I cried.

"Nay, Smith Galwyn!" Master Glebus said, his round face kind but his tone firm. "We go to war, and you've a skill that's needed. Many a man and many a horse will fall before this fight is over. There are many ways of serving Lord Artos." He turned me around and pushed me toward the door.

I did not wish to go to sandal the horse whose owner had kept me from saving my pony. But Master Glebus eyed me more sternly now.

"We'll do what's necessary here, Smith Galwyn." And with that use of my title, he reminded me that I had duties that must be honored.

"You will guard Cornix?"

"With my life," answered Eoain, one hand on his knife hilt, his expression resolute.

BERICUS AND THE PRINCELING met me halfway across the stableyard.

"Galwyn," Bericus began. He was frowning and his manner reproving. "What meant you—"

"Iswy has been here. He killed Spadix because he couldn't kill Cornix."

"What?" Bericus rocked back on his heels, his expression altering to concern. "Is that why the gates were closed? Iswy? Here?"

"In Cornovian colors," I repeated once again, and continued to stride toward my forge and this princeling's needy horse.

"I know his face," Bericus said. "I'll help in the search. He must be found. Lord Artos needs Cornix."

"Oh, *he'll* be guarded well enough," I said in such a savage tone that Bericus gave me a sharp look. I didn't care. "If Iswy had ridden Cornix to Deva, this wouldn't have happened."

Bericus paused, then said in a kinder tone, "But Iswy *couldn't* ride the stallion." He turned to the princeling. "Galwyn's news requires urgent action, Prince Maldon. You must excuse me. The smith will tend your horse now."

I did, for that was my responsibility; and the horse had immediate need of my skills, his off-fore so badly worn by travel that I had to build up the outside edge of the sandal to compensate. Prince Maldon said nothing, and he walked off shortly, leaving his groom to hold the warhorse. Borvo and Maros, two of Master Ilfor's apprentices, appeared not long after. From the quick look I gave them, I could see by their expressions that they knew about the killing.

I WORKED THROUGH THE NIGHT. Borvo and Maros, who had been among those watching my first display for Master Ilfor, now forged sandals that I then fit to hooves.

Bericus stopped by to say that a full search for Iswy was under way in Camelot and in the main Cornovian encampment down below.

"Iswy will not escape us," he promised me. "And Cornix and all the other war stallions are being close guarded."

I nodded and went back to work. Iswy had already

escaped or was hiding where he was unlikely to be found. Of that I was certain.

But somehow I would find him. I didn't believe he would rest until he killed Cornix, too. I had no doubt that he would try again.

As the cock crowed that dawn, I had the feeling that I must have shod half the horses in Lord Artos's army. I hadn't, but before I could, Master Ilfor entered my forge and hauled me off to my bed. A soldier followed and took a position at my doorway. So the shoer and the shod were all being guarded.

"I'll wake you if there are any problems," he said, and I think I was asleep before he left me.

IT WAS CLOSE TO MIDDAY, from the way the sun was shining in, when I was gently shaken awake by another soldier to tend the lame horse of one of the Atrebatii princes. He had not been shod, so it was not precisely my expertise needed but Master Glebus's. Still, the bounds of traditional duties blurred in emergencies. I roused Borvo, asleep on the floor by my pallet, and we examined the footsore animal.

The horse had split his hoof to the bulb of the foot and it would be weeks before he was sound again. I trimmed as much as I could and contrived a sandal that would relieve pressure on the sorest point of that foot, putting another plate on his right hoof to balance him.

"But what shall I ride to the battle?" I was asked.

"I heard that replacements are being brought in from nearby farms," I said, for Borvo had mentioned that sometime the previous evening.

Three more warhorses arrived. Borvo, Maros, and I stopped long enough to eat and then were back to work. Even those who had been skeptical of the benefit of the iron rims decided their horses required them—now!

AND THEN, SUDDENLY, preparations were as complete as possible. A high mass was said that evening for the success of the endeavor; all the lords received the sacrament and special anointings and blessings from the religious community. Everyone who could cram his body into the chapel was included in the final blessing, and certainly in the prayers of all those who would stay behind.

The next morning, at false dawn, shriven, anointed, and blessed, Lord Artos and his Companions mounted their black steeds in the courtyard. The ladies tied favors onto their lances.

Lord Artos himself had no wife yet, though a prestigious marriage was rumored. No doubt, when news of his victory came, the family would be all too willing to align themselves with the *dux bellorum*.

Borvo and Maros were mounted on two halfbreed Libyans big and sturdy enough for such hefty men. I, of course, had Ravus, who was quivering with excitement. Even our two pack ponies, laden with tools and iron bars, were fractious.

We stood to one side as the *Comes Britannorum* led his Companions toward the main road. For once it was empty of its usual traffic.

I don't know who was more surprised, myself or

Cornix, when he was hauled back on his heels and those behind Lord Artos nearly ran up his back.

"*Galwyn Varianus*," bellowed my lord, pointing his gloved hand at me. "*What are you doing . . . there?*"

I looked about me stupidly.

"Take your position instantly"—and now he pointed to where Bericus, Bwlch, Bedwyr, and Drustanus were trying to control the cavortings of their Libyan stallions. "I want you where we can watch out for you," he said, making me aware that he knew what had happened in Cornix's stable. "The others are to fall in behind my Companions. Immediately behind my Companions." And he scowled at me when I was too startled to move. "*Now!*"

Ravus moved almost without my urging, as if he felt he knew where he belonged, and Bericus grinned back at me.

"No hoof, no horse!" he exclaimed, eyes dancing with mischief.

I felt cheered for the first time since Spadix died.

THE EUPHORIA OF OUR DEPARTURE lasted us well into the day, with only brief stops for horses to rest and men to relieve themselves. We ate in the saddle at the walk. Otherwise we traveled at a good trot, the foot soldiers in the dust behind us but keeping up with the horses for all they had only two legs to go on. I wondered fretfully if Iswy were among them.

The second day, after a night checking loose sandals, I caught what rest I could in the saddle. Once again I blessed Ravus's smooth gaits. But because I slept on horseback, I scarcely recall much of the journey, though I do remember people cheering Lord Artos with "See the black horses! See the big, beautiful black horses!"

I was checking Cornix's hind plate the night we camped outside Ratae when the messenger came galloping up to Lord Artos's tent.

"The Saxons have crossed their borders, *Comes*." The messenger's voice was hoarse but loud enough to be heard around the camp. "I am to tell you that Aelle and his sons have gone east to Bannovalum. He must turn west, though, to avoid the fens at Metaris Aest."

"Then we'll march to Durobrivae, to Cnut's Dike, and head north along that until we meet these scurrilous invaders," Lord Artos said. "Inform your prince. Blwch, see that this man is fed and provided with a fresh horse."

Blwch left with the messenger and I finished the stallion's hooves. Cornix was picketed right by Lord Artos's tent—the other Libyans nearby, in the most protected area of the camp. Cornix was in good fettle but he would often neigh wistfully. It would cause my breath to catch in my throat—that he still missed his pony companion. And where was Iswy now?

THE NEXT DAY'S LONG MARCH did get us over the rolling countryside to Durobrivae by late evening. The next morning, we turned north until another messenger arrived. I wasn't close enough to hear what he had to say but Lord Artos seemed very glad of his information, laughing and grinning as he called in his Companions.

Once again I spent the night with Borvo and Maros,

checking all the war steeds, though only two needed to have clinches tightened. The camp was not still. I do not think many slept, for the rumors were that we were closing with the Saxons.

I heard other messengers arrive during the night; the spring evening seemed to amplify the sound of hurried hoofbeats.

We moved eastward well before dawn, making our way to a position above the confluence of two rivers. We were on a long slope above them, and they were not in full spate.

"The Saxons are there," I heard Bwlch murmur to Cei. Then the Companion saw me. "Galwyn, you and your smiths stay out of the battle line, but be handy." He pointed to a slight knoll behind us and, dutifully, I motioned the others to follow me as I led Ravus there. The tools in our saddlebags clinked softly against the nails and spare sandals.

Thus it was that Borvo, Maros, and I had probably the best view of the first Battle of the Glein. We spotted the Saxon force crossing the upper river, hundreds of them, with their winged helmets and their huge round shields. More poured from the opposite bank, wading through the knee-high water. The Saxon horde paused when suddenly our line of archers spread out on the hill crest. I could hear the black horses whinnying—but out of sight below the brow of the hill.

I didn't know much about battle strategy in those days but I certainly trusted Lord Artos's wisdom and foresight. Had he not equipped himself and his Companions with the black horses? Had he not met the

Saxons before they could achieve their objective: the domination and control of all East Anglia?

Audible now were the war cries of the Saxons as they swarmed up the hill to meet the waiting Britons. I heard the angry hiss as our archers loosed their arrows, to rain down on the oncoming foemen. And then I saw our mountain men step up beside the archers, and watched their lethal showers of stones knock men to their knees.

Still the Saxons charged forward, bellowing fiercely, in a seemingly endless flow across the river, multiplying the force opposing us. Their shouts all but drowned out the neighs of the Libyans.

And then, just when the Saxons were halfway up the hill and the barrage of our arrows and stones had thinned, the black horses moved up and over the brow of the hill, Artos on Cornix in front.

The black stallion reared, pawing the air with his metal-rimmed hooves. I *saw* the shock and horror on the faces of the leading Saxons. I *saw* them halt in their tracks as more and more big black horses followed Artos and charged down at them.

I shall never forget that sight—as frightening as I had once imagined it would be, those years ago during my first visit to Camelot. And I was not an enemy suddenly faced with the flaring red nostrils, the bared teeth, the *blackness* of these monsters. I was not a Saxon with no way to evade flashing, iron-clad hooves.

I cheered loudly, pumping my right arm skyward in a salute to that charge and leaning just slightly to my left. And heard, and felt, something zing past me between arm and head.

I whirled, crouching, hand on my dagger hilt, wondering what missile had so narrowly missed me.

Iswy was already launching himself at me, face contorted, dagger raised. He didn't even see Borvo and Maros instantly coming to my defense.

"No, he's mine!" I shouted at them, and ducked away from my assailant. "He slaughtered my pony!"

I didn't think of Yayin's lessons in dagger fighting: I thought only of avenging Spadix. That lent me a cunning I didn't know I possessed. I noticed that I had the reach of Iswy, for I had grown in arm as well as leg, and the years at the anvil had matured the spindly cabin boy Iswy had once mocked.

He came at me again and I caught his dagger hand, forcing it back, hoping to break it; but somehow he squirmed free and sliced at my belly.

The leather apron I had put on that morning deflected his blade. He cursed wildly.

"I'm not the easy mark I used to be, Iswy." It was my turn to taunt him as we crouched, facing one another and circling, each trying to discover an opening.

Like a snake, he twisted and made to stab at Ravus where the gray was tied to a bush. But Ravus reared, breaking the restraint and trying to run. Maros, for all his bulk, was fast on his feet and caught the trailing reins.

"Horse killer!" I cried. "That takes such a brave man, doesn't it, Iswy? To kill an animal that looks to be protected by you!"

I changed my dagger from hand to hand, making him watch the transfer: a trick Yayin had drilled me in. Then I attacked, just as I had switched the blade once more to the left. Iswy didn't expect that and didn't know which way to lunge. I sliced at his right leg, catching him above the knee with a deep gash.

He staggered back, totally surprised by my strategy. I switched the blade again even as I closed with him, my left hand gripping his right wrist and arm. I struck downward, through this leather jerkin, and into his chest.

"You've—killed—me," he gasped out, sinking to the ground, dead before his body stretched out.

I looked down at him and did not close his sightless eyes. Spadix's death was now avenged. Still gasping from my exertions, I turned away, back to the battle raging on the slope below.

The Companions on the great black horses wielded their swords tirelessly and brought down every Saxon enemy they passed on their way to the Glein. The river was turning red in the sun, with the blood of the wounded and dying.

And then our reinforcements—the troops of half-breed Libyans—charged out of the woods from the left of the river. It was a total rout of Aelle's arrogant horde.

"That were well done, Master Galwyn," said Borvo at my side.

"That were some fight," Maros added.

They were looking at the carnage below, but it wasn't that battle they meant.

"There," I said, pointing to a loose horse, limping badly and dazed as it wandered back up the hill. "We must be about our duties."

We left Iswy's body where it had fallen, where the ravens would find it.

THAT WAS THE FIRST Battle of the Glein, and the only one I fought in. As Master Glebus had said, I had a skill that was of far more service to Lord Artos than that of another swordsman's.

There were twelve great battles in all, the final one at Mount Badon. But though I lifted neither dagger nor sword in any other, I played my part, watching every one of them, and keeping well shod the great black horses of Artos, the *Comes Britannorum*.

AFTERWORD

Although farriery as a profession was not established as a guild in England until 1160, under Baron de Fer, horseshoes as such were used even in Caesar's days. The Worshipful Company of Farriers is still going in Hereford, training up masters in the art to shoe the horses of today for their various tasks.

Unfortunately iron does not last well, so few examples of early horseshoes—or sandals, as they were indeed called—have been preserved. However, it is true that a blacksmith was an extremely important craftsman, since he made weapons for defense as well as other important tools.

It is also very true that the Libyan horses that Arthur is reputed to have bought in the horse fair at Septimania would have had foot problems, carrying the weight of large, well-armed men and moving over surfaces different to the ones in their native country. Though Hollywood would have us believe fifth-century knights wore full-body suits of armor, they actually used only breastplates, and leg and arm guards such as the Roman soldiers had, and carried heavy swords and shields. That gear alone required big, strong horses to bear them any distance. Such weight, as well as the uneven and wet terrain, would have caused hoof problems. Britain in those days tended to be wetter and warmer than it is now.

I feel it is reasonable that horseshoes would have had to be developed for the purpose of keeping Arthur's cavalry sound. "No hoof, no horse" is still a farrier's truism. And there would have needed to be men knowledgeable about hooves and iron, to make such aids.

It is historically true that someone like Artos, a *Comes Britannorum* and *dux bellorum* (war leader), existed in the latter part of the fifth century and the early part of the sixth century. This leader united the tribes of Britain to defend themselves against the Saxons invading from their base at York. I prefer to keep to the historical facts, such as they are, in this extrapolation. These facts include the strong Roman and Christian religious practices current in those times.

I have not included Merlin in this story because he is not historically mentioned by contemporary chroniclers, namely Gildas and Nennius, who are reputed to have lived when Artos did. Nor have I bothered resetting the age-old triangle of Arthur, Guinevere, and Lancelot. Arthur is not thought to have married before the first of his great battles, when his fame would have made him a fine match. Guinevere is purported to have come from a prestigious family of Roman Celts, and marriage with Arthur would have enhanced her family's reputation as well as shown support to his efforts.

Since this is my story, about a facet of those times, I

can deal with such facts as I choose from those available. But all the farriery details have been checked by Master Farrier Joseph Tobin, Associate of the Worshipful Company of Farriers, and those facts concerning horses in general by my daughter, Georgeanne Kennedy, Irish Certificate of Equine Sciences and British Horse Society Assistant Instructor.

The reading I did on my own.

Dragonhold-Underhill
Wicklow County, Ireland, 1995

Dragonmen must fly
when Threads are in the sky!

THE MASTERHARPER OF PERN

In a time when no Thread has fallen for
centuries—when, indeed, many are beginning to dare hope that Thread will never
fall again—a boy is born to Harper Hall.
His name is Robinton, and he is destined
to be one of the most famous and beloved
leaders Pern has ever known.

THE DRAGONRIDERS OF PERN®
by Anne McCaffrey

Published by Del Rey® Books.
Coming in paperback to bookstores everywhere
December 1998!

❧ FREE DRINKS ❧

Take the Del Rey® survey and get a free newsletter! Answer the questions below and we will send you complimentary copies of the DRINK (Del Rey® Ink) newsletter free for one year. Here's where you will find out all about upcoming books, read articles by top authors, artists, and editors, and get the inside scoop on your favorite books.

Age _____ Sex ❑ M ❑ F

Highest education level: ❑ high school ❑ college ❑ graduate degree

Annual income: ❑ $0-30,000 ❑ $30,001-60,000 ❑ over $60,000

Number of books you read per month: ❑ 0-2 ❑ 3-5 ❑ 6 or more

Preference: ❑ fantasy ❑ science fiction ❑ horror ❑ other fiction ❑ nonfiction

I buy books in hardcover: ❑ frequently ❑ sometimes ❑ rarely

I buy books at: ❑ superstores ❑ mall bookstores ❑ independent bookstores
❑ mail order

I read books by new authors: ❑ frequently ❑ sometimes ❑ rarely

I read comic books: ❑ frequently ❑ sometimes ❑ rarely

I watch the Sci-Fi cable TV channel: ❑ frequently ❑ sometimes ❑ rarely

I am interested in collector editions (signed by the author or illustrated):
❑ yes ❑ no ❑ maybe

I read Star Wars novels: ❑ frequently ❑ sometimes ❑ rarely

I read Star Trek novels: ❑ frequently ❑ sometimes ❑ rarely

I read the following newspapers and magazines:

❑ *Analog*	❑ *Locus*	❑ *Popular Science*
❑ *Asimov*	❑ *Wired*	❑ *USA Today*
❑ *SF Universe*	❑ *Realms of Fantasy*	❑ *The New York Times*

Check the box if you do not want your name and address shared with qualified vendors ❑

Name _____
Address _____
City/State/Zip _____
E-mail _____

mccaffrey/black

PLEASE SEND TO: DEL REY®/The DRINK
201 EAST 50TH STREET, NEW YORK, NY 10022 OR FAX TO
THE ATTENTION OF DEL REY PUBLICITY 212/572-2676